# ATLANTIS RISING

## THE AEGIS OF MERLIN BOOK 8

### JAMES E WISHER

*James E. Wisher*

SAND HILL PUBLISHING

Copyright © 2019 by James E Wisher

All rights reserved.

No part of this book may be reproduced in any form or by any electronic or mechanical means, including information storage and retrieval systems, without written permission from the author, except for the use of brief quotations in a book review.

Edited by: Janie Linn Dullard

Cover art by: Paganus

101220191.0

ISBN: 978-1-945763-64-9

## PROLOGUE

*Child of Atlantis, we need you!*
Merik sat up in bed, his heart racing in the dark. His sheets were a soaked, tangled mess wrapped around his legs. How many times had the nightmare woken him this week? Every night it felt like, though the memory slowly faded throughout the day. The details were vague, but that last, desperate plea never changed. Child of Atlantis, what did it even mean? Atlantis was a fairytale. The sort of thing you told your kids about at bedtime.

Merik was nearing forty. Why would he be dreaming about something so childish? Like every other morning, he had no answers. He'd fallen asleep with the tv on and it was playing highlights of the Four Nations Tournament. It seemed the boy wizard had made quite a splash on the first day of competition.

He sighed, switched it off, and flicked a glance at the cheap digital clock sitting on the equally cheap motel nightstand beside his bed. Four o'clock. If he went back to sleep now, he'd feel worse than if he just got up.

Kicking the sheets off his legs, Merik rolled out of bed and stretched. Ten days on the road usually left him eager to return home, but not this trip. Ireland was nice, but that wasn't why he hated to end the trip. All he had waiting for him was a divorce paper in need of signing. He held no illusions about the future of his marriage, but that didn't mean he was eager to end it. At least there were no kids to argue over. They'd sell the house, split the money, and go their separate ways, like the last ten years hadn't happened.

The short carpet was rough on his bare feet as he shuffled across the room toward the cramped bathroom. He flipped the switches and an overhead fan whirred to life. As the water slowly got warm, he stared at his reflection in the mirror. His eyes were dark from lack of sleep, but he still had all his hair and only one chin. He wasn't a horrible catch, was he? He traveled a lot for work but made good money. Surely he could find a new girlfriend even at his age.

His vision blurred for a moment and when it cleared his reflection showed someone different. It was still him, but with three gems embedded in his forehead and more woven into a nonexistent beard.

Merik rubbed his eyes. Was he having a stroke?

*Come to us. We need you.*

The voice from his dream echoed in his mind. Merik had met two wizards over the years, both haughty women that wouldn't give a nobody like him a second glance, but he'd never experienced real magic until now. At least he assumed it was magic and not that he was losing his mind.

"Who are you? Where are you?"

*We are the people of Atlantis and we are trapped. You who share our blood must save us.*

Merik was an exotic meats exporter from Sentinel City. His family had left the Kingdom of the Isles four generations ago.

His lineage was the blandest, most boring thing anyone could imagine. Nothing about it suggested magic of any sort.

"I think you've got the wrong guy."

*No. So few of us remain. We cannot be mistaken. The recessive is dominant in you. Time grows short. Come to us and all will be made clear.*

Merik had finished all his meetings for this trip, why couldn't he take a little side adventure? After all the stress he'd endured over the past year he deserved it.

"How do I find you?"

*Travel northwest. You will know when you're close.*

"Then what?"

The presence was gone, vanished as if it had never been. Northwest would take him toward the Atlantic Coast. That made sense; if he was looking for Atlantis, naturally it would be near the ocean, or perhaps under it. He shrugged and got into the shower. At the very least the drive should be nice and maybe it would clear his mind.

A little over an hour later the sun was up and Merik was on the road. The most directly northwest road was a narrow, two-lane country track. His rental SUV had a full tank of gas, so at least he shouldn't end up on the side of the road before he reached wherever he was going.

The Emerald Isle lived up to its name. He drove past fields of the greenest grass he'd ever seen, filled with cows munching away. On a sales trip he'd usually never bother with a side trek like this. Time was money after all. Eventually the farms grew less and less common and the road rougher. Two lanes eventually became one and a half. If Merik met a truck, he didn't know what he'd do.

But he didn't meet any trucks. He didn't meet anything at all. He could have been alone in the world.

At last, three hours of driving brought him to a wide-open

turn-around spot on a cliff overlooking the ocean. It was the most beautiful place he'd ever seen. Waves lapped at the rocks below and a light, salty breeze off the water flowed through his rolled-down window. He would have liked to stay until sunset but hadn't brought a picnic lunch.

He parked and got out of the car. The instant he did, he felt something, like the voice in his dreams, but different. A quick look around revealed a path leading north about thirty feet from the cliff's edge. That was the way he was supposed to go. He set out at a quick walk.

Branches hung low over the dirt trail forcing him to constantly duck. He shivered. It felt twenty degrees cooler under the canopy. The pressure in his mind urged him to hurry, not in words but just with a feeling. The difficulty of the hike forced him to take his time. He didn't want to end up on his face after all.

At last he reached the end of the trail, a wall of rock easily ten stories tall. What caught his eye was the cave entrance at the base. That had to be what the presence wanted him to find. If he'd known spelunking was in his future, he would have brought a flashlight. He considered and rejected making a torch. His outdoor skills were nonexistent. Merik couldn't make a fire to save his life unless he had a lighter and kerosene. And even then, he was apt to burn himself.

*Hurry!*

"Alright, alright."

He walked to the cave entrance. It was awfully dark in there. Maybe if he trailed his hand along the wall and moved slowly…

Merik crossed the threshold and twenty feet ahead of him a crystal flared to life, filling the tunnel with cool, blue light. He grinned. Maybe he really was on the trail of Atlantis.

He kept going for a good ten minutes before he finally

glanced back. The tunnel was so dark he might as well have been in another world. He shivered but kept moving.

Twenty minutes after entering the tunnel he reached a large chamber lit by a crystal in the ceiling as large as he was tall. Below it sat a trio of stone tables, each with a metal chest on top. He rubbed his hands. Maybe there was gold inside.

First, he opened the left-hand chest. Inside was a display of six gray crystals each the size of his pinky. The right-hand chest held a single red crystal about the size of an egg. If he was going to find any real treasure, it would have to be in the central chest.

Holding his breath, Merik eased the lid open. His hand trembled. Inside were the three crystals from his dream. The ones he'd had in his forehead. Below them were four smaller ones that matched what he saw in his beard, as well as another pair that were as clear as glass.

All his dreams were real.

The dark blue central crystal pulsed with energy. He picked it up and placed it in the center of his forehead. There was no pain as it fused with his flesh, only a slight tightening of the skin.

*Welcome, brother.*

The voice from his dream was stronger than ever in his mind. What would happen when he added the other two crystals? Time to find out. Merik took the second crystal and touched it to his forehead, just to the right of the central shard.

No reaction. It felt cold against his skin. A dead piece of stone where the first felt warm and alive.

*Your flesh can only harmonize with a single crystal at a time.*

"How long until I can add the rest?"

*It is different for everyone. Perhaps days, perhaps weeks. You will know when the crystal feels warm in your hand. For now, you must gather all the items and leave this place. The dogs of Lemuria will already be on their way.*

Merik hurried to collect all the crystals, stuffing them into his pockets as fast as he could. "How could anyone know I'm here?"

*This place is a trap. Much Atlantean blood has been spilled here.*

"Why bring me here if it's a trap?"

*Because without these items, you can't complete your mission and bring back Atlantis. Escape the hunters and you can succeed. Die and the trap will be reset for the next unlucky Child of Atlantis.*

Merik liked his situation less and less. What had been an exciting adventure was getting sketchier by the moment. "Can I do anything with the crystal to fight back?"

*The one you wear has already made you stronger and tougher than an ordinary human. Having the gray crystals on your person will protect you from the dog's magic. Beyond that you have only your resourcefulness and will to rely on.*

"Great."

With the last crystal in his pocket, Merik started back up the tunnel. It was as silent going up as it had been coming down. Exactly what resourcefulness was he supposed to rely on? He was a traveling salesman for a meat processing company for god's sake. Merik had never even been in a fistfight. The closest thing to combat he'd ever encountered was high school football. And the gridiron wasn't a battlefield, despite what their coach liked to say.

Merik tensed when the light of the tunnel entrance appeared. His pace slowed until he came to a dead stop twenty feet from the exit. Would there be killers out there waiting for him? Given the madness of the day, he'd be crazy to dismiss the possibility.

After half a minute of indecision he straightened his shoulders and strode out into the clearing. A single figure stood facing him. Of average height and slender build, the stranger didn't look terribly imposing. Of course, the dark cloak covering him from shoulders to ankles and the deep cowl hiding his face obscured most of the details. All Merik could see was a pair of black boots and a double-edged sword blade that angled across his waist to point at the ground.

"Hi," Merik said. God that sounded stupid. "I don't suppose we could go our separate ways and pretend we never met?"

"No." The sword rose to point at him. When it did, he got a look at the figure underneath. And what a figure. Her blue shirt and gray pants snuggly wrapped a slim but still very feminine body. "Atlantis will not rise again. Not on my watch. Gust!"

A sudden wind picked up dirt and gravel and shot them at Merik, blinding him.

*Duck!*

He dropped to his knees.

The assassin's sword passed so close to his head he felt the breeze.

When he scrambled to his feet, they'd exchanged positions. She now stood between him and the cave. He held no illusions about his ability to outrun her. The woman had to be at least fifteen years younger than him and she looked like she worked out. What he couldn't figure out was why she didn't have a gun. She could have put two in his chest the moment he appeared and been on her way.

*Your crystal generates a kinetic barrier. It will stop bullets or arrows, but not a sword. Too much mass.*

That was helpful, assuming he didn't get his head cut off.

"You dodged my blade once," the assassin said. "You will not do so a second time."

Merik believed her. He couldn't outrun her or outfight her. That left only one option.

He turned and sprinted for the cliff.

She was right on his tail.

As soon as the edge was in view he leapt.

The water glistened below him.

Way below.

Hopefully those physical enhancements the voice mentioned would keep him alive.

---

Merik came sputtering out of the water and stared up at the top of the cliff. The assassin was gone. He'd feared the woman simply leaping in after him. In truth he couldn't imagine why she didn't.

*Her sword would be less effective in the water and the anti-magic properties of the gray crystals would render her magic ineffective. She will likely track you and seek a better opportunity to finish what she started.*

"You're a barrel of good news. How can she track me if the crystals stop magic?" Merik started swimming north, away from his car. If the assassin wanted to find him, that was a probable place for her to start looking.

*For those that know how to look, you appear as a void in their magical perception. Most wizards would never think to search for such a thing, but a Hound of Lemuria will certainly be aware of the effect. Nonetheless you should be proud. You are the first Child of Atlantis to escape the guardian of the cave.*

"Wait, everyone else you sent was killed by that girl?"

*"Not her specifically, rather her predecessors. It's been thirty years since the last attempt to secure the crystals.*

Merik grunted and focused on swimming. He could feel the difference the crystal's magic was making on his body. Before, he would have been exhausted by now, but with the extra power he hardly felt winded. By following the steep cliff that marked the water's edge, he eventually reached a small, secluded beach and pulled himself out of the water.

There wasn't a soul to be seen, but a narrow animal path led away from the ocean. With no better options he followed it into the woods. Walking with your clothes plastered to your skin wasn't a pleasant experience, but it beat getting your head cut off. He just wished he had some idea where he was and how to get back to civilization.

"What, exactly, am I supposed to do now?" Merik asked.

*You must break the spell that has held us in stasis for these many millennia. The key to bringing Atlantis back to the mortal realm is the large red crystal you retrieved. You have heard of Stonehenge?*

"Sure, everyone's heard of Stonehenge."

*The stone circle was constructed by the Lemurians around a crystal pillar that serves as the door to Atlantis. When the red crystal is brought inside the circle, the pillar will appear. There is an obvious indentation where it fits. Placing the crystal will restore the pillar, allowing Atlantis to return.*

"Then what?"

*We are few in number thanks to the curse placed upon us by our ancient enemies. We will need to make contact with the leaders of this age. Those that can be swayed to our service will be supported and given power. Those who refuse will be replaced with more willing partners. Atlantis will be the puppet master of this world. And you will be a hero of our people.*

Merik grinned. No one had ever called him a hero. He liked the sound of it.

After an hour of walking, the roar and rattle of a passing truck caught his attention. The road couldn't be that far away. He turned toward the noise and left his nice trail to beat a path through the woods. Lucky for him, the undergrowth wasn't that thick and his crystal protected his skin from scratches and scrapes.

At last, a little after noon, he stepped out of the forest and onto the edge of the road. The nearest civilization would be one of the farms he'd passed on his way in and they were miles away. He needed his car but feared encountering the assassin again.

She couldn't exactly murder him in front of witnesses. He pulled out his cellphone and said a short prayer that it had survived his swim. The manufacturer claimed it was water resistant, time to find out if they were all talk.

He swiped the phone to life and let out a long sigh when the home screen appeared. He'd have to leave a nice review when he got to a computer. Even better, by some miracle, he had a signal. Not a great signal, but good enough to call roadside service. They'd send him a cab.

He paused before dialing. "How do I hide this crystal? Anyone that sees it is going to get curious."

*You need only wish it to be invisible and it will be to all save those with the blood of Atlantis.*

That solved that problem. Merik commanded the crystal to disappear. Two hours later a black-and-green taxi pulled up and Merik got in.

"What the hell happened to you, mate?" the driver asked, making no mention of the stone embedded in Merik's head.

"Long story. My car's just a few miles up the road. I was too exhausted to take another step."

The drive didn't take ten minutes. His car looked fine and there was no sign of the assassin. Once his car was running, he waved at the cabby, turned around, and followed him back to town. It seemed his guess about the assassin was right. She didn't want to attract any attention. Still, he harbored no illusions that she'd given up. As he made the walk to his motel room, he could almost feel her eyes on his back.

🜛

Clean, dry, and dressed in fresh clothes, Merik sat on the motel bed and laid out his full collection of crystals. His personal group sat on one side. Cold, smooth, and inert, they showed no sign of being ready to join the first one on his forehead. The six gray, magic-negating crystals and two clear ones rested on the opposite side while the large red one glittered in the center.

It would probably be easiest to drive to Stonehenge, but that would leave him vulnerable to the assassin. Maybe a bus or train would be better.

*You cannot enter the circle of stones. The Lemurians' magic prevents anyone with Atlantean blood from approaching.*

Merik frowned. "Then how am I supposed to free you?"

*A dupe must be found. One with no connection to Atlantis and stupid enough to carry out your instructions without too much thought.*

Merik scratched his head. Maybe he could pay a tourist to do it. No, they'd be sure to ask questions he didn't want to answer assuming whoever he approached didn't think he was a lunatic. He'd have to find someone with the correct mindset.

*We have been trapped for thousands of years. There is no need to rush. Best to do it right the first time. You must also seed the world with both the anti-magic and the detection crystals. Give them to those that fear and hate wizards as much as we do, preparing the way for our return.*

"Who should I give them to? I don't know anyone that could do anything useful for your cause," Merik asked.

*We leave that to your judgement. Our knowledge of the mortal realm is limited. Just make certain to keep one to protect yourself.*

Merik didn't need to be told twice. What he did need was to start making plans and doing research. Bringing back Atlantis was going to be a far more complex task than he'd imagined. But he would do it.

Hero of an entire race. That sounded much better than traveling salesman.

His wife said he'd never amount to anything. He grinned. This would show her once and for all who was a failure.

CHAPTER 1

The two arms of the motorcycle's front fork glowed as Conryu used earth magic to shape the prongs into a decorative twisted pattern. The weather on the floating island was perfect today, a light breeze blew and the sun shone down through a clear sky. He was happy to work outside. Behind him a simple shop constructed with magic had a sign over the door that said Koda Chrome. He'd always wanted his own place and now he had one.

Since the madness two months ago with the Le Fay Society, Conryu had only visited Sentinel City to pick up his mother for a regular, short lunch. They didn't eat in the city, instead he'd open a portal to London or wherever she wanted to go. The North American Alliance made it clear that they wanted him under their control. He made it equally clear that he wasn't interested in being anyone's pawn. They had a warrant out for his arrest should he appear anywhere in North America.

Not that anyone had the guts to try and enforce it. One of the advantages of being the most powerful wizard in the world was that people tended not to bother you. Still, he saw no reason to push his luck. Better to avoid the place altogether.

When the forks looked the way the client requested, he snapped his fingers, ending the magic. Another gesture sent the fork floating up into the slot on the bike's front end. The best thing about magic was that he didn't need a hydraulic lift. The whole chopper floated in front of him at the perfect height. He sighed, tightened the bolts, and lowered the bike to the ground.

Done. He'd deliver it this afternoon and collect his payment along with any new projects that had come in.

"Are you really going to use your magic to play mechanic for the rest of your life?" Maria Kane, the most beautiful girl he knew and the love of his life, stood with crossed arms glaring at the motorcycle like it was the bike's fault he wasn't following her preferred course. She wore her white robes and a gold belt at her waist that contrasted perfectly with her jet-black hair. "You could do so much more."

"Sure I could." Conryu wiped his hands on his jeans and picked up the Staff of All Elements. The artifact allowed him to use magic without spells as well as access his private library. "But should I? I could run around, trying to solve all the world's problems, but I'd probably just make new ones. I figure the best thing for me to do is mind my own business."

She snorted. "Like that's going to last. You're too important to be allowed to just hang around here. You should at least come back to the Academy with me and finish senior year, get your degree. I'm sure the teachers would welcome you."

"And how long before the military showed up to try and take me into custody? No, thank you. When do classes start again?"

"Day after tomorrow."

"Want me to drop you off early? I'm on my way to deliver the bike anyway."

"I guess. You'll pick me up for our Sunday date though, right?"

Conryu grinned and kissed her. "Wouldn't miss it."

He pointed the staff at an open patch of grass a few feet away and a moment later a door with a knocker that looked like a bearded old man appeared.

"Prime!" Conryu said. "Quit sulking and get over here. We're leaving."

A black book with an impossibly huge, fang-filled mouth glided over beside him. His familiar had been in a sour mood since it became clear Conryu no longer needed to learn spells. With the staff, he could shape magic at will into whatever form he desired. That didn't mean he didn't appreciate everything Prime had done for him. Without the scholomantic he wouldn't have survived the past three years.

"A being of my magnificence doesn't sulk," Prime said.

"What do you call it?" Conryu asked.

"A period of melancholy. I'm over it now."

"Good. Kai, watch the fort. I'll be back in a couple hours." His personal ninja-slash-bodyguard was currently watching over him from the border of Hell, but she would have no trouble hearing what he said.

As he and Maria made the short walk to the library doors she asked, "Kai lets you out of her sight without a chaperone now?"

"If I promise not to do anything dangerous."

Conryu opened the door, looked back, and pointed at the finished motorcycle. A light magic force field appeared around it and lifted it off the ground. Galen, the spirit that served as the librarian, didn't like it when Conryu got oil or grease on the floor. It didn't matter that it vanished with a thought. The idea of making a mess in the room seemed to offend the ancient spirit.

He willed the bike to fly in ahead of them, Maria followed it, then Conryu closed the door behind them. Inside, the familiar bookcases stretched in every direction. Only the smell of parchment was missing. Since the books were just physical manifestations of Galen's memory, they had no smell and little weight compared to their size.

The only new addition to the library was a case that held a dozen elf artifacts he'd collected. Since he was the only one that could access the library, this was the safest place to store them. Maria had been studying them off and on this summer, but had made little progress.

"I'll drop you at the Academy before I head to London."

Maria nodded and sighed. "This will be the first time we've been apart in a while. It's going to be strange not having you just a few floors away."

"You've got the rune stone I prepared, right? If there's trouble, you can contact me at any time. I'll be there quick as thought."

She hugged him. "I know you will, but it still feels different. But enough talking. If we're going to do this, let's get on with it."

Conryu pictured Maria's room in the dorm and willed the library doors to open. Beyond them was a modest two-bed unit with minimal decorations. Three suitcases sat beside the bed nearest the door. Her parents had shipped them ahead since she wasn't arriving by train. Her roommate wouldn't get there until tomorrow, which made this a safe place to drop her off. One of the teachers was bound to notice his presence, but he'd be gone before anyone could reach her room.

"I'll miss you," Conryu said.

"You could always stay," Maria said.

"Not a chance. See you Sunday."

She gave him a final kiss and stepped out of the library. Conryu waved and shut the doors. It was just him and Prime for a while now.

He glanced at the demon book who said, "I'm not giving you a kiss."

Conryu barked a laugh and pictured the alley behind Pop's Wheels, the London bike shop that he subcontracted for.

🝓

Conryu left the library, sealing the doors behind him. As soon as he was clear, he dispelled the force field surrounding the bike and pushed it toward the loading dock at the rear of Pop's shop. The clatter of machinery filled the air. London was under major construction after the damage Morgana caused. Even with all their resources focused on it, Conryu doubted the city would be back to normal for years.

He placed the staff out of sight in a pocket dimension. Prime flew along beside him, entirely indifferent to what anyone might think. That supreme confidence, you might even say arrogance, was one of the few things he envied in Prime. Much as he liked to pretend otherwise, Conryu hated disappointing people.

The door to the workshop was open and a familiar figure stood staring at a bike that had seen better days. In fact, judging by the amount of rust covering the engine, Conryu doubted it had run in his lifetime. Pop liked to buy old bikes and fix them up for resale. The custom work Conryu did for him was just a bonus.

"Hey, Pop."

The old man turned and smiled through his grease-stained

beard. He wore a leather apron that had two pockets overflowing with tools and a pair of old battered black boots.

"Done already, Conryu?"

"Yeah, see what you think." Conryu pushed the bike up the ramp, put down the kickstand, and leaned it over.

Pop walked all around it, nodding to himself. "Gorgeous work as always. I should have brought on a wizard years ago."

Conryu grinned. There probably wasn't another wizard that would bother with this kind of work. They could make so much more money in so many other ways with their magic, it wouldn't make sense. Conryu did it because he loved it, not for the money. Pop reached into a pocket and pulled out a roll of hundred-pound notes which Conryu accepted.

"Got anything else for me?"

"Not this week I'm afraid."

"Want to join me for some fish and chips?"

"No can do. I've got to make a little progress on this rusted-out piece of junk."

Conryu shrugged. Pop never joined him for lunch, but Conryu always offered. "See you next week then."

Pop waved and went back to contemplating his new project. He wasn't going to make much progress that way, but it wasn't Conryu's place to say so. Pop did things his own way at his own speed and that was just the way it was. He must have had money socked away somewhere.

He left the old man to his work and walked back down the ramp. His favorite chip shop was only two blocks east. After a quick bite he'd head home and work on his own project, a motorcycle made completely using magic. It would be a first he felt certain.

"Conryu."

He winced at that voice; his vision of a quiet afternoon

puttering gone in a flash. "Jemma. I don't suppose you're here to join me for a plate of fish and chips?"

"No. A matter has come to our attention. I'm hoping you can help."

He turned. Jemma St. Simon was the head of the Kingdom's Ministry of Magic. She'd aged since the last time he saw her and that was only a month ago. Her eyes were streaked with red and her skin had an unhealthy pallor. The black robe that marked her as a dark aligned wizard was crisp at least and her hair was tied back in a neat braid.

"What's the problem this time?" he asked.

"It might be best not to discuss this sort of thing out in the open. Never know who might be listening."

Conryu looked around. Other than a lost Yorkie, they had the street to themselves. Everyone was either working or at lunch this time of day. Not that it mattered. He'd get nothing out of her until she felt at ease.

With a thought he summoned the staff and opened the library doors. "I trust this will be private enough for you."

"It will do."

Inside he willed a pair of chairs into being and dropped into one. "Let's have it."

She sat more daintily and said, "You remember the True Face of God cult?"

Since they were the first batch of lunatics that tried to kill him, he wasn't apt to forget. "What are they up to now?"

"Murder, specifically burning future wizards at the stake."

"That's nasty even for them, but hardly unusual. Why is the Ministry interested?"

"Somehow the cultists have found a way to identify potential wizards as young as thirteen. A new test. We have no details, but if it's true and not just more of their mad propaganda, it would be a remarkable breakthrough."

"If it's that important, why not send a team of your own? I know you have magic ops teams. Surely they could get whatever it is you need."

"I'm sure, but there's the matter of getting government permission. You see, if there's one thing that gets the bureaucrats in a twist, it's interfering in another county's internal affairs. They're afraid that if we do it, someone else will feel free to stick their noses in here. Despite the fact that they're a murderous theocracy, they're still the government. Which brings us to you."

Conryu rubbed the bridge of his nose. "I hate politics. I left the Alliance because I didn't want to be used by them. What makes you think I want to be used by your government?"

"Hate us all you want, but it doesn't change the fact that innocent girls are getting burned alive. We can't make a difference, but you can. And if you should learn the secret of how they discover the girls at such a young age, I'm willing to buy it for fifty thousand pounds. Save some lives and make some cash, win win." Jemma looked longingly at the library shelves. "As long as we're here, I don't suppose I could take a look?"

"Nope." The door appeared at his command. "I'll think over your offer."

When she'd returned to the London street and Conryu sealed the library Prime said, "She's not telling you everything."

"Of course she's not. Jemma's as secretive as any other government official. She is right about one thing. If innocents are being killed, I have to try and help. Galen."

The ghost of a bearded wizard appeared before him. "Chosen?"

"Ever heard of a way to identify a wizard before she turns eighteen?"

"No, though as I've told you repeatedly my knowledge isn't total."

"Thanks." Conryu willed the library back to his floating island.

First he needed to find the girls, then he'd figure out how to save them. If he got the information Jemma wanted, well, he wouldn't turn down fifty thousand pounds.

## CHAPTER 2

Professor Angus McDoogle sat in the small office at the rear of his apartment and read his latest royalty statement. Sales for *Merlin Reborn* had dropped by half since Conryu left the Alliance. No one liked being told what to do, but you'd think the boy would have a little consideration for Angus's position. All Conryu's bad press was killing sales of his book.

He tossed the paper aside and it landed on the pile of bills covering his desk. He'd been so certain that when his theory was mostly validated, a teaching position would open up for him, but no, the deans were all jealous of his success and refused to give him a chance. No doubt they feared he'd upstage them.

He'd shown them all once and he'd do it again. Angus needed a new project. One that didn't involve ungrateful children. If Conryu didn't appreciate all the publicity Angus had generated for him, let him handle his own PR from now on.

Angus stood, stretched, and walked to the two overloaded bookcases that covered one side of his office wall. The titles were a mixture of scholarly texts and more theoretical pieces. This one about the Tibetan Yeti had potential. No one had yet proven definitively whether the creature existed or not. But that would require him to travel to the land of the Iron Emperor and the immortal ruler of China wasn't known for his hospitality when it came to outsiders.

Perhaps another subject. His gaze wandered over the spines as he waited for inspiration to strike. In the end it was the doorbell that brought his search to a close. He wasn't expecting any guests. As a matter of fact, he hadn't even had an interview offer in weeks.

Curious now, he left the office, walked through his living room, and unbolted the door. Standing outside was a delivery man in a brown uniform holding a box perhaps six inches square wrapped in white butcher paper in one hand and a clipboard in the other.

"Angus McDoogle?" the man asked.

"That's Professor McDoogle. Can I help you?"

"Delivery." The man held out the clipboard. "Just need you to sign by your name."

Angus hadn't ordered anything and seldom received fan mail. He shrugged and signed. Maybe whatever was in the box would jar him out of his funk.

"There you go. Good afternoon." The delivery man handed him the package and marched off with that determined stride they all seemed to use.

Angus closed and locked the door again before retreating to his office. His settled in his chair and took a letter opener out of the top drawer. A minute and some grumbling and swearing later and he found a finely crafted wooden chest, like a mini pirate treasure chest. Even if it was empty, it would make a fine collectable.

The lid went silently up and inside he found a neatly folded letter and a crimson gemstone the size of his thumb knuckle. A ruby that size would be worth a fortune, so he doubted that's what the stone was. He smoothed the letter and started reading.

*Dear Professor McDoogle,*

*I'm a huge admirer of your Merlin book and wanted to make a suggestion for your next project. I assume a man as learned as you has heard the legend of Atlantis. The lost island is an obsession of mine, but much like the legend of Merlin, most people don't take it seriously. I hoped that if a person of your stature were to discover the truth, the world would be forced to take it seriously. If you're interested in learning more, you'll find a map on the back of this paper.*

Angus turned the letter over and found nothing but a blank, white page. He frowned and returned to the message.

*To reveal the map, you need to take a flashlight and shine it through the crystal. The red light will make the image clear. Please forgive the secrecy, but I wouldn't want anyone else claiming this find before you.*

*Your devoted fan,*

*M*

Angus wasn't usually keen on this sort of cloak-and-dagger business, but he couldn't deny a certain excitement. He'd never given Atlantis much thought. As the letter said, it was regarded as a legend. He overlooked it just like everyone else. Given his past, maybe he shouldn't have.

Excited now, he hurried out to the kitchen and rummaged through his junk drawer until he found a flashlight. With the letter on the counter and the stone held to the flashlight's lens he switched it on. Red light spilled over the paper like a puddle of blood. Immediately the outline of a map appeared along with latitude and longitude numbers.

Angus grinned like a little boy at Christmas and rushed back to his office to find an atlas. He had his project now.

Everyone would see that he was more than just a one-trick pony.

꩜

After his conversation with Jemma, Conryu returned to the floating island. It was only midday, so he had plenty of time to begin scouting. The problem was, the True Face of God cult controlled a huge territory. He wasn't sure where to begin. If she was so worried, you'd think Jemma could have given him an address at least.

He stepped out of the library near his workshop and took three steps before Kai appeared and bowed. His bodyguard was dressed in all black as was her habit, the hilt of her sword jutting over her shoulder. At least she hadn't bothered with a mask. Long hair framed a pale, narrow face.

Kai bowed. "Chosen, you appeared troubled."

Despite his best efforts, Conryu had yet to convince her to call him by his name rather than his title. She'd tried for a while but looked so uncomfortable he stopped asking.

"I got some news today and I'm not sure what to do about it. No, that's not right. I know what to do, I'm just not sure how best to go about it." He looked at Kai for a moment and nearly slapped his forehead. "You said there are a bunch of ninjas where you come from, right?"

"Nearly a hundred when I left, all devoted to serving you should you wish to call on them. You never gave any indication that you did."

"Up until this moment, I didn't. Now I don't have a choice. Can you take me to them?"

"Of course. We'll have to travel through Hell though. It's the only way I know to get there."

Conryu shrugged. He hadn't gone for a ride on Cerberus for a while. It would be a nice change of pace.

An hour later they were racing through the black emptiness of Hell on the back of his guardian demon. Cerberus followed Kai's directions perfectly. After a rough first meeting, the two of them now got along well. Since they both wanted to protect Conryu, it made sense for them to be friends.

"Stop here, Chosen," Kai said.

Conryu slid off Cerberus's back and looked around at the endless nothing. How did she know for sure? He neither saw nor sensed anything to indicate where they were.

"Are you sure?" Conryu asked.

"Yes, I have been here many times. Focus on the darkness and reach out. If I can feel the presence of my sisters, you will be able to as well."

He'd never been very good at this sort of subtle magic. His specialties ran toward blowing things up. Maybe just thinking he was bad at it was what blocked him. Conryu frowned and focused fully on the flow of dark magic through the area. The gem on his staff turned black in response to his request.

A few seconds later he felt them, dozens of weak, dark aligned wizards just beyond the veil that separated the mortal realm from Hell. He really needed to practice more.

Conryu patted Cerberus on the flank. "Good job, boy. I'll try to visit more often. Maybe next time we can hunt some demons."

Cerberus gave an eager bark and licked his face. At least the demon dog's tongues were dry.

Conryu opened a portal and he and Kai stepped through.

The first thing he noticed was the heat and humidity. They were in the center of a clearing marked by a ritual circle. Palm trees towered over them and a narrow, winding path led into the jungle. A sweet perfume from unseen flowers filled the air.

He didn't have a chance to enjoy it as ten women dressed like Kai appeared out of thin air all around them, swords drawn and crackling with dark magic.

"Trespassers are not welcome here," one of the women said. "Prepare to return to Hell."

Not exactly the greeting Conryu had expected. He tapped the ground with his staff and released a pulse of dark magic that sent the women flying.

Before they could recover Kai said, "You dare greet the Reaper's Chosen with bare steel? Be grateful he doesn't kill you all for such disrespect."

Conryu winced. Kai knew him well enough by now to know he'd never kill anyone over such a small thing. With his power, there was no chance they'd actually hurt him. But maybe she knew her audience better than he did. The ninjas scrambled to their knees and touched their heads to the ground.

"Forgive us, Chosen," the one who made the threat earlier said. "We did not know you at once."

In unison all ten raised their heads and leaned back, exposing their throats. "Our lives are yours."

"Thanks, but I need live help not corpses. Who's in charge anyway?"

"That would be Grandmaster Narumi," Kai said.

"Alas, it is no longer," the spokeswoman said. She waved her hand and the other nine vanished. "The grandmaster fell in battle three weeks ago. I have taken her place until a new grandmaster can be elected."

Kai fell to her knees. When she spoke, her voice trembled. "Impossible. How? The illusion protects us. If you don't know the way here, the island is inaccessible."

"The barrier fell a month ago. A week after that, the first wave of the Iron Emperor's stone soldiers marched out of the ocean and onto the beach. We've been fighting them off and on ever since. Fully a third of our order has fallen, including the grandmaster."

"Who are you?" Conryu asked.

"Forgive my rudeness, Chosen." The woman removed her head wrap. "My name is Kanna. Grandmaster Narumi was my mother. In her name and my own I pledge our service and if need be our lives to you."

She was older than Kai by about fifteen years. Her eyes were dark and hollow from worry. Sunken cheeks and thin lips gave her a drawn-out look. Clearly the stress of her current situation had taken a toll. Conryu suspected under better circumstances she would have been beautiful.

He was about to ask another question when a gong sounded repeatedly.

"They come again," Kanna said. "On the north beach. I must go."

She vanished into the borderlands.

Kai leapt to her feet. "We should help."

"We will. Then you'll have to tell me what the grandmaster meant to you. That was the strongest reaction I've ever seen you make."

Conryu raised his staff and summoned the winds to carry them skyward. He turned north and soon after reached the beach. Stone statues carved to look like medieval warriors dressed in armor and carrying spears marched out of the surf. Kai's sisters met them with black steel. Their dark-magic-charged blades sliced easily through the stone soldiers, but the loss of a limb didn't bother the constructs and more came every second.

"Let me down, Chosen," Kai said. "I must fight with my sisters."

"No need. The core of those constructs is filled with magic. I can dispel them all in a moment."

Conryu slashed the staff and a wave of darkness rolled out, washing over the ninjas without effect only to slam into the statues and snuff out their cores. The dark magic kept going, driven by his will, until he had destroyed all the constructs underwater as well.

He and Kai landed on the beach and everyone immediately took a knee.

Conryu glanced at Kai. "Are they going to do this every time I show up?"

She actually cracked a smile. "At least until they get used to you."

"Is anyone hurt?" he asked.

Kanna stood. "Not this time, thanks to you, Chosen. We should have at least a few days and perhaps a week before they strike again. You needed us for something. Please, tell us how we may serve."

"My problem will keep for a few hours. Do you have wounded from earlier battles?"

"Seven are in the infirmary, too injured to fight. Others have minor wounds that don't keep them sidelined."

"Take me to the infirmary." She started to fade into the borderland. "On foot, please. You can fill me in on what's happening."

Kanna returned to solidity. "As you wish. The village isn't far. Follow me."

He and Kai fell in beside Kanna. As they walked, she told them of the barrier's weakening and eventual failure. Not long after, the stone soldiers appeared. They'd been fighting off waves of the constructs ever since.

"Why does the Iron Emperor care about your village?" Conryu asked. "Have you attacked the Empire?"

"No," Kanna said. "But we do grant sanctuary to any dark aligned girl that wishes to escape. That's something he can't accept. It's a sign of weakness."

They reached the edge of a small village. There was a longhouse on one side of the clearing, a handful of smaller buildings, and a central well. He'd never seen a place this low tech.

"You seem to know a lot about the Empire," Conryu said.

"I do. My mother was one of the girls granted sanctuary and she told me all about it. I will die before I allow any of us to be taken back. The infirmary is this way."

She led him to a thirty-by-thirty building directly across from the longhouse. The only door was a blanket hanging across the entrance. Inside, seven of the ten beds were occupied by women with horrible injuries. One was missing an arm; another had a bandage covering half her face.

When he entered, the sole healthy person knelt and the rest tried to rise from their sickbeds. "Stop that. Everyone relax."

It was easy to forget that they didn't have access to light magic healing. Everyone on the island was dark aligned after all. That said, they were all still human and healing magic wouldn't hurt them.

Conryu went to the nearest woman, really a girl he guessed couldn't be over nineteen. She'd lost her left arm from the elbow down. Her blond hair was sweat plastered to her head. He reached out and took her good hand. Light magic flowed into her and over the next few seconds her arm regenerated.

When he sensed no more damage, he moved on to the next person. Conryu repeated the process for each of the wounded. When he was finished, he turned to find all of them out of their beds and on their knees, heads touching the floor. Kanna had joined them, leaving only him and Kai still standing.

"Okay, respect is one thing, but I have no wish to be worshiped. Everybody up."

They stood and Kanna dismissed the newly healed. When they'd gone, she said, "Are you certain you're the Chosen of Death? I've read the histories and all the others were cruel, merciless women that desired nothing beyond power and adoration. Certainly none of them would have gone out of their way to heal the wounded."

"If I'm supposed to be your leader, I wouldn't be a very good one if I let my people stay hurt, would I?" Conryu rolled up his sleeve so she could see the scythe mark on his forearm. "I assure you the Reaper marked me. It's not something I'll ever forget."

"I didn't mean to doubt you, Chosen," Kanna said. "Will you restore the illusion now?"

"I'm not too good at that sort of magic. Besides, the Iron Emperor knows where you are. Even if I hid the island, his stone soldiers could march right through the illusion. No, we need to find you all a new home. In the meantime, I have an idea about how to hold off the constructs. Prime?"

"Yes, Master?"

"Do you know how I might go about raising an anti-magic wall around the island and making it last for a while?"

Prime sniffed. "Certainly, Master. Raising the wall will be simple enough for you. To make it last, you'll need to open a Hell gate in the center of the island and connect the dark energy to the wall. You'll also have to ward it to keep any demons from coming out."

"You know how to construct the ward?"

Prime just stared at him.

"Of course you do. Sorry I asked."

"Chosen?" Kanna said. "I'm sorry to interrupt, but will you appoint a new grandmaster to oversee the village?"

"I thought you all voted on that."

"Usually, we would, as long as there was no Chosen to appoint one. Since you're here…"

Conryu glanced at Kai who nodded. "Fine, you seem to be doing a good job. If no one objects, I'm okay with you continuing to do it."

"I am honored by your confidence. Will you oversee the ritual of investiture?"

He badly wanted to say no but sighed and nodded. "When will you have it?"

"Midnight tonight."

"Alright, that will give Prime and me time to prepare the anti-magic barrier. But tomorrow we leave for Europe."

## CHAPTER 3

Jonny Salazar grimaced as his black leather boots sank into the sand up to his ankles. Somehow the miserable stuff always found a gap. He'd be itching for hours after his patrol. And the heat, goddamn. His desert camo uniform felt like an oven when the sun was pounding down on him.

The beach stretched for miles in every direction, beautiful, fit people as far as the eye could see. Beach patrol was everything he'd ever imagined and then some, minus the sand. And he had Conryu to thank for it. The brass had heard how helpful he'd been in taking down the crazy wizards that attacked Sentinel City and after he graduated offered him this sweet post.

He'd been on duty for a month now and hadn't shot a single zombie. He also hadn't gotten a single date. Everything you heard about women liking a man in uniform turned out to be bullshit, at least in his experiences so far. Jonny remained ever hopeful that given the sheer number of babes down here, he'd find one that was interested. He certainly wasn't going to stop looking.

Speaking of looking, a bronze beauty went bouncing by, her bikini barely covering her lean body.

"Private Salazar! We're here to look for zombies not to drool over the tourists." Corporal Keen, his training officer, bawled Jonny out at least three times a day when his gaze wandered. The guy was in his midtwenties, looked like a model, and had a general for a father. He probably didn't need to look for girls, they no doubt threw themselves at him. Must be nice.

"Sorry, sir! The scenery is distracting. I'll try to do better."

"You've been saying that every day since you arrived. Time to stop talking and start doing your job."

*Jackass.* "Sir, yes sir!"

They'd barely taken a step when a high-pitched scream rang out from the waterline. Jonny drew his service pistol and ran after Corporal Keen.

He dodged around fleeing men and women, for once taking no notice of the bodies passing him by.

Jonny's heart raced and his breath came in ragged gasps.

This was it.

His first contact with the monsters that he was sworn to destroy.

He scrambled to a stop and stared at the two rotted creatures shuffling up out of the surf. Their eyes had long since been eaten by fish, the sockets now filled with an unnatural glow. Sections of bone were exposed in their arms and face. What little clothes they wore hung off them in torn strips.

His pistol snapped up and he took aim.

"Steady," Corporal Keen said. "Let them get away from the water. The burn crews will thank you for it."

The zombies finally noticed Jonny and his superior. The creatures let out a low moan and stumbled toward them.

Jonny backed up until they were clear of the surf and put a bullet in each of their foreheads. The zombies dropped and didn't move again.

"Kind of anticlimactic." He holstered his pistol. After the crazy shit he'd seen with Conryu, this was nothing to get excited about.

"Yes, well, the real terror comes when we get back to base and have to fill out all the paperwork. Keep watch and make sure no more show up. I'll call in the burn crew."

Jonny kept his hand on the butt of his pistol for the hour it took the burn crew, which consisted of a guy with a flamethrower, a guy with a shovel, and a guy with a box of heavy-duty black bags, to arrive, but the bodies never twitched. A bullet to the head was enough to kill a zombie just as well as a man after all.

The nasty stink of highly flammable fuel filled the air along with a stream of flames. The whole process, from incineration to cleanup, took another two hours. By the time it was taken care of, Jonny and Keen had reached the end of their shift. They caught a ride back with the cleaners.

In the back of the truck with the burned-up remains Jonny yawned and stretched. Somehow he'd imagined his first encounter with the undead would have been more exciting and less ordinary. It seemed impossible to become jaded in a month, but he was working on it.

It had taken most of the day and evening for Conryu and Prime to finish the barrier surrounding the island.

Following Prime's instructions, the task had been simple enough, just time consuming. As they worked, his mind would drift occasionally to the girls in danger of being burned at the stake. Hopefully this extra day wouldn't condemn any more innocents to death. For all his power, he couldn't be in two places at once and he owed these women something for their unasked-for devotion.

Conryu sighed and shifted on an uncomfortable throne made to look like it was built out of bone. The ceremony to officially make Kanna grandmaster of the Daughters of the Reaper was taking place in the longhouse. The women's cots had been pushed up against the wall leaving most of the single, large room empty. A black carpet ran the length of the room and on either side of it, all the ninjas knelt, their heads touching the floor.

And they were all naked. Sixty-six fit, attractive woman, thirty-three on either side of the carpet, faced him. At least in their current position all he could see was their backs and the tops of their heads. Conryu had summoned the Reaper's Cloak and transformed the staff into a scythe. Beside him, Kai stood, fully dressed in her black uniform with her sword on her back. She had argued at first that it wouldn't be appropriate for her not to take part as a regular sister, but Conryu overruled her. Seeing her naked wasn't something he couldn't unsee and since they were together every day he figured it was best not to take chances.

"Not a word about this to Maria," he said.

"The ritual isn't sexual, Chosen. I'm sure if you explained, Maria wouldn't be upset. We perform the investiture naked and unarmed because that is how we all face death in the end."

"You tell Maria that I was in a room with almost seventy naked women and I'll be the one facing death. Now let's get this over with."

As if summoned by his voice, the door opened and Kanna, naked as all the others, stepped into the room. She walked calmly down the carpet, her steps making hardly a sound. At the end of the carpet she knelt and all the others raised their heads to witness the final portion of the ritual.

Conryu stood, pointed his scythe at Kanna, and recited the words as he'd been instructed. "Do you swear your life and soul to the Reaper's service and your loyalty to me, his chosen representative on earth?"

"I do," Kanna said.

"Do you swear to lead your sisters with strength and honor until death claims you?"

"I do."

"Then rise, Grandmaster Kanna, and take your place at my side."

She rose and moved to stand beside him. Kai draped a black cloak over her shoulders and the gathered ninjas let out a cheer. Conryu kept his gaze locked on the floor. If he was going to be able to face Maria the next time he saw her, the fewer sights he took in the better.

When Kanna at last dismissed her followers Kai said, "It's safe now, Chosen."

"Thank goodness." He dismissed the cloak and scythe. "You need to look after yourself. I don't want to have to do that again."

Kanna smiled; it was the first real expression he'd seen on her stern face. "According to the histories, the other Chosen always had an orgy after the ritual."

"You're messing with me, right?"

"Perhaps a little, but that doesn't make it any less true. Now, before the others return to prepare for sleep, what do you wish us to do for you?"

"I need you to scout the country under the control of the

True Face of God cult. It used to be Spain; I don't know what they call it now. They're burning young wizards at the stake and I mean to put a stop to it. I also need to know how they're finding the girls so early. Once you've located all the imprisoned girls, we'll rescue them in one fell swoop. Anything else risks the others being killed once word reaches their captors."

Kanna looked from him to Kai. "You're right, he is different. The healing partly convinced me, but this mission confirms it. We'll be ready to go in the morning, Chosen. Before you leave allow me to say it is an honor to serve you."

She bowed and walked away. Conryu summoned the library and entered with Kai and Prime. When the doors had closed he asked, "What did you tell her?"

"While you and Prime were working, Kanna asked me about our adventures and what sort of master you were. I told her all that we had done and that you weren't my master, you were my friend. I don't think she entirely believed me, at least not until now. My sisters through the years have served many Chosen, all of them monsters that used and discarded us like animals. To serve a kind, honorable master is more than any of them dreamed possible. It was more than I dreamed possible until I met you."

"Why do they serve people unworthy of them?"

"You heard the oath. We serve the one chosen by the Reaper. It is not our place to question the will of a god. Loyalty will see us reborn at Death's side as black angels for eternity. Disloyalty gets an eternity of punishment."

"I knew the Reaper was a jerk the moment I met him." Conryu willed a pair of beds into existence. "Let's get some sleep. Tomorrow's going to be a busy day."

Merik stroked his beard, gently brushing across the four crystals woven into it. The sun had barely risen and he was watching the approach to Stonehenge from a comfortable distance, waiting for his dupe to arrive and activate the pillar. He wasn't worried about the assassin that had confronted him last year when he claimed his birthright. The voice in his mind explained that the purpose of the beard crystals was to mask his presence. It wasn't totally effective, but unless she was within a few yards of him, Merik would remain unnoticed by her magical senses.

He'd learned and accomplished a great deal in the last year. No longer was he an out-of-his-depth salesman. He understood both his new power and his purpose. He had a destiny now, an important one. Having that to focus on had a profound impact on him. The weak, uncertain man he'd been was nothing but a memory. If his wife could see him now, she might not even want a divorce.

Someone appeared on the path. Merik smiled. The pompous professor at last. The moment he read Angus's book about Merlin, he knew the old man would be the perfect one to complete his mission. He was too arrogant to ever imagine that he was being used. He'd only see the glory and leap to seize it.

As Angus made his way closer to the circle of standing stones, Merik's smile vanished. He raised a hand and concentrated.

The moron hadn't brought the crystal with him!

Without that, the pillar wouldn't appear and he couldn't activate it.

Merik calmed himself. This wasn't a disaster. Despite his appearance, Angus was clearly an intelligent man capable of figuring out what was wrong. When nothing happened, he'd retrieve the crystal and try again. No need to worry.

A moment later the assassin appeared out of thin air behind Angus.

Shit! If she got a hold of Angus, the old professor would tell her everything.

*The Lemurian dog must not gain possession of the key.*

Merik didn't need to be told that. He left Angus and the woman to their discussion and hurried back toward the village. He'd been tailing Angus at a distance since he arrived and knew exactly where he was staying. The power of his crystals allowed him to run at full speed over long distances without getting winded. At a dead sprint he reached the edge of Ames in only five minutes.

He slowed to a walk and approached the inn. There was a line of people waiting for a table at the restaurant so he used a side door. The staff was all occupied with the breakfast rush which suited him perfectly. A quick dash up the stairs brought him to Angus's room. The door was locked.

Merik concentrated on the left-side crystal embedded in his forehead. This one gave him limited telekinetic power which he used to manipulate the tumblers and open the door. A glance up and down the hall indicated that no one had noticed his unauthorized entry.

Inside, the room was neat, with all the professor's clothes still folded in his suitcase. Merik didn't care about Angus's packing habits. He sensed the crystal's unique vibration coming from the wall safe. It was a combination-style safe, which was easily dealt with by his enhanced senses of touch and hearing.

Merik pocketed the crystal and made himself scarce. It wouldn't take long for Angus, the assassin, or both if she decided not to kill him, to return. While he no longer feared the woman like he had, Merik had no desire for another altercation. It would only serve to draw attention he didn't need.

What he did need was to find a new dupe as quickly as possible.

# CHAPTER 4

Angus woke in the small inn he'd chosen in the town of Ames just a mile from Stonehenge. He never imagined he might be in the Kingdom of the Isles again so soon, much less to investigate one of the Kingdom's most famous mysteries. It was lucky that after all the help he gave them, the government restored his travel privileges. When he determined the circle of stones' true purpose, his former colleagues would turn green with envy.

He grinned and leapt out of bed. There was nothing like a mystery to get one's blood pumping. Aside from its convenient location, the main reason Angus chose this particular inn was that each room had a safe. No sense carrying something as valuable as the red crystal around with him until he determined its purpose. He opened the safe once more and found the crystal still in its box exactly as he left it. Satisfied that it was as secure as it could be given his limited options, Angus left his room, ate breakfast in the bar, and called a cab to take him to Stonehenge.

When he arrived, he found the site free of tourists and

rubbed his hands. Just as he hoped. The casual visitors weren't up this early. He should have an hour or two before the crowds gathered to pose beside the megaliths and take pictures. It was almost a crime against history to let the ignorant masses run their hands over the ancient stones and trample the grass like a herd of sheep. Oh well, it wasn't like they could do any damage to the massive rocks.

Angus made a slow circle around the standing stones but found nothing that looked like an opening for the crystal. There were no pictographs, runes, or anything else to give him a clue. He paused and thought. There couldn't be anything obvious. If there was, someone else would have found it by now. Assuming someone hadn't sent him on a wild goose chase, what was he missing?

The answer hit all at once. The crystal obviously needed to be here for whatever he was supposed to find to appear. Like the hidden map on the back of the letter, a beam of red light played over the stones would show him the way. Leaving the crystal behind had been the cautious move and he generally took that route if possible, but this time it appeared to have backfired on him.

He shrugged. There was nothing to do but head back to the inn, retrieve the artifact, and try again.

Angus turned and found himself facing a young woman dressed in a dark cloak with the hood thrown back. Young and pretty, she was exactly the sort of girl an old man like him might like to run into, except for the sword. She held a sharp, straight blade bare in her hand.

"I knew if I waited long enough the Atlantean or one of his servants would show up. You will lead me to your master or I'll kill you where you stand."

Angus stared at the woman, trying to process her threat. Nothing she said made any sense. "I think you have me mistaken for someone else. I serve no master, though I am researching the theory of Atlantis for my next book. I'm Angus McDoogle. Perhaps you've heard of me?"

He blinked and she closed the distance between them. Her sword was cold where it touched his throat. "Do not imagine you can lie to me. You have been in contact with Atlantean crystals recently. Their stench covers you. I will ask you once more and only once more. Where is your master?"

Everything clicked into place for Angus. "Wait, please. I received a red crystal in the mail along with a fan letter recommending Atlantis as the subject for my next book. I was directed here to learn more. I swear I have no idea who sent the package."

She looked deep into his eyes. It felt like she was judging his soul. Finally, she stepped back. "I believe you. The Atlantean is clever, using you as an intermediary. You can tell me nothing because you know nothing."

He winced at being told he knew nothing, but in this case was content to let it go. "So I can keep my head?"

"Yes, but you can't keep the crystal. You will take me to it and hand it over. I suggest you return home and forget all about Atlantis. It will be good for your health."

Angus swallowed hard. What had seemed like a dream project had turned into a nightmare. His desire for glory was reduced to the simple need to survive.

"The crystal is locked up in my room. Shall we go?"

Half an hour after he left, Angus was back at his inn. The dining room was filled with the breakfast crowd, all of them happily and noisily chatting as they devoured scones, bacon and eggs, sausage and beans, and all washed down with tea or coffee. The smells filling the air made Angus want to pull up a chair and indulge in a second breakfast of his own. Alas he doubted his unwelcome companion would stand for the delay.

He made straight for his room, waving to the proprietress who frowned back when she caught a glimpse of the young woman with him.

At the top of the stairs he said, "I fear you've ruined my reputation."

"You're still breathing, aren't you?" she countered.

It was a fair point. He made the short walk to his room in silence. Angus took out his key and frowned. The door was open a fraction. He remembered locking it and testing the door before he left this morning. He considered the possibility that the cleaning staff was inside, but the quiet made that unlikely.

"What is the problem?" the young woman asked.

"The door's open already. I fear my room has been burgled."

She pulled him aside, pushed the door open, and drew her sword as she stepped inside. Angus peered in past her. The room was empty, but the safe had been opened. Even from a distance it was clear the crystal was gone.

His companion crossed to the safe and made a mystical pass in front of the open door. "He was here, minutes ago. God damn it! Somehow he always stays a step ahead of me."

Angus had no idea what to say and further angering the young lady with the sword seemed imprudent, so he stayed silent. Inside, his mind raced to make sense of everything he'd learned. The only thing he was certain of was that he'd gotten drawn into something far bigger than he'd suspected.

"I must return to Stonehenge," the woman said. "The Atlantean is forbidden to enter the stones, but he will find another to take your place before long."

"Wait! What am I supposed to do?"

She cocked her head. "Whatever you like, just stay away from my prey. Should you throw in with the Atlantean, I will be forced to consider you an enemy. And you do not want to be my enemy."

With that she vanished, leaving him alone in his room.

Angus sighed. Maybe Atlantis wouldn't be the best subject for a book after all.

⁂

Even with a force of sixty-six ninjas able to move instantly through the border of Hell, scouting an area the size of Spain wasn't a quick task. Conryu had set up his base in an abandoned monastery overlooking the Atlantic Ocean. The building only had half its roof and the pews were long since rotted to nothing, but it made a handy place for Kanna and the others to come back to and report in.

As they worked, an image of the True Face of God cult's activities was building. On a stone table Conryu conjured out of the floor he had a map of the area. Apparently, the priests were working their way north and south from the country's center where they'd built a massive building that was half church, half palace and the home of their supreme leader. That meant the cultists had at least two devices capable of detecting wizard potential in the young girls. It was a complication, but not an impossible one.

"What do you think, Prime?" he asked.

"I think that helping these girls does nothing to increase your personal power and if you were a demon, you'd be better off either searching for more artifacts or mastering new magic. You clearly have no intention of doing either of those things, so I'll just say that it's more interesting than watching you play with the motorcycles you so love."

"Well, as long as you're amused that's what matters. You

know, these girls we're saving will grow up to be wizards and they'll be in my debt. Doesn't that increase my power?"

"It would if you had any intentions of manipulating them to your benefit, but you don't. As a demon, you would be a massive failure."

Conryu grinned. That was the best compliment Prime had ever given him, even though the scholomantic clearly meant it as an insult.

A slight tremor ran through his magical perception and a moment later Kanna appeared and bowed. They'd arranged things so that all her subordinates reported to her then she reported to him. That suited Conryu fine as keeping track of sixty-six ninjas wasn't a task he wanted.

"How're we doing?" he asked.

"Good, Chosen. We've located thirty-two girls awaiting execution and one of the two priests handling the tests. According to their report, the medium is a clear crystal to which blood is applied. The crystal then turns color to match the girl's alignment, assuming she has magical potential."

"That's similar to the device they use at the Academy to sort the students by alignment. How much of the country remains to be searched?"

"I believe another day will do it," Kanna said. "I've prioritized finding the second crystal."

"Good. If they can't identify the girls, then they can't execute them."

There was a second tremor and one of the ninjas appeared beside Kanna. "Forgive me, Chosen, but one of the girls is going to be executed in thirty minutes."

"Shit! We haven't located the second crystal yet." Conryu stood and ran a hand through his hair. He couldn't let an innocent girl burn, but without that second crystal, the hunt would never end.

"The priests leading the search are planning to oversee her execution," the second ninja said. "They probably have the crystal with them."

"Okay, I'd planned to handle this quietly, but I guess we'll need to go with plan B. Kanna, rally the troops and get them in position to free the girls we've found on my signal. I'd prefer to do this without casualties, but don't take any unnecessary risks. If some lunatic cultist gets in your way, do what you must."

"Yes, Chosen." Kanna vanished to organize things.

Conryu pointed at the second woman. "You. What was your name?"

"Melina, Chosen."

"Okay, you and Kai are with me. How many girls are being held with the one about to be executed?"

"None. She was the only one they found in the nearby village. The little I heard indicated that some of the villagers tried to hide her and the priests found out. They're gathering everyone to show them what happens to those that disobey."

"Charming. Let's have a look at this village."

Melina disappeared into the borderland and Conryu joined her. Kai was waiting along with Cerberus who let out a happy bark. Conryu patted his flank. The demon dog had learned that Kai and her fellow ninjas were friendly and no longer tried to devour them when they approached. A fact that the ladies were no doubt happy about.

"After you, Melina."

It was a short journey through the endless darkness. "Here, Chosen."

Conryu willed a viewing window into being. A medieval village, complete with thatch-roofed houses and dirt streets, appeared. A tall, gaunt man in white robes and wearing a gold crucifix stood with crossed arms watching as a grim group of villagers built a mound of firewood around a cross in the town square.

The image shifted and he soon found a girl about thirteen dressed in a simple white shift tied to a stake at the edge of the square. Her blond hair was matted with blood and her right eye had begun to swell shut. Someone had given her a working over. Conryu would very much like to know who that someone was so he could introduce himself with a roundhouse kick.

"I'll get the girl. Where does he keep the crystal?"

"There's a tent at the edge of town," Melina said. "Guards watch it, so I believe the crystal's in there."

"Can you sneak in and find out for sure? If it is there, grab it now."

Melina bowed. "As you command, Chosen."

She sprinted away leaving Conryu to figure out how best to extract the girl and make sure the priests understood that burning innocent girls at the stake wasn't acceptable.

"You've gotten comfortable with commanding the Daughters," Kai said.

He grimaced. "Not really, but I can't do this on my own, so I'm adapting. Like I said, I'm not looking to be in charge of anything."

"It wasn't a criticism," Kai said. "You can't imagine how satisfying it is to have a worthwhile mission. I know the others feel the same."

"But if one of them gets hurt or killed following my orders… How am I supposed to live with that?"

"You live with it by knowing that she died doing her duty, a duty she chose long before she met you. We are warriors, Conryu. Death's most favored after you. Dying is not something any of us fear."

"Thanks, Kai."

Cerberus stiffened, alerting him to someone's approach. A moment later Melina appeared. He held out a clear crystal and bowed. "No one saw me, Chosen."

"Outstanding." He took the crystal and cast a simple divination on it.

The crystal didn't register as magical. He tried earth magic, but the spell failed, indicating it wasn't made of stone. He frowned and prepared another spell.

Before he could cast it, Kanna appeared. "All are in position, Chosen."

Research would have to wait. He pocketed the stone. "Good."

He focused and they flew upward until the viewing window appeared a few hundred feet in the air. "I need to make an impression on these assholes so they stop murdering innocent people. I doubt it will take for long, but I still have to try."

They watched through the portal until a pair of burly guards grabbed the girl and dragged her toward the cross. That was his cue. "You three stay out of sight."

With that Conryu stepped out of Hell, cast a flying spell, and called out to the wind spirits. A storm of vengeance was about to wash over these monsters.

## CHAPTER 5

Thunder cracked and lightning flashed all around Conryu as his conjured storm grew in power. The wind roared and funnel clouds began to form. Below him, the gathered cultists and villagers stared up at the sudden change in the weather. He pointed and a lightning bolt crashed into the ground fifty feet from the gathering.

That got their attention. Everyone scattered. The head priest and his guards broke for the nearest building.

Conryu pointed again and a second lightning bolt lanced out, striking directly in their path. They weren't getting away that easily. The guard dragging the future wizard to her execution gave up and let her go. The girl fell to her knees and put her hands over her head.

That was enough for the preliminaries. He sent a pulse of dark energy out to signal the others before conjuring a massive tornado that fully engulfed the village square.

Conryu landed beside the girl and held out a hand. "Are you alright?" His light magic translation spell sent the question directly into her mind.

She looked at him with wide eyes for a moment before nodding and letting him help her up.

"Monster! Abomination!" The priest screamed obscenities at them. "Children of Satan! We shall send you back to Hell where you belong!"

The guards pulled pistols. Before they could fire, he turned the weapons to rust. They stared stupidly at what was left of their weapons. Conryu gestured and the guards collapsed, leaving only the priest facing him.

He closed the distance between them, grabbed the gaunt man by the front of his white cassock, and dragged him close enough that their noses were almost touching. "I'm only going to say this once. Your witch hunt is over. You hurt one more innocent girl and I'll come back and burn every church in this miserable country to the ground with you and your comrades in them. Do we understand one another?"

"We do God's work," the trembling priest said.

"You do someone's work, but it isn't God. Remember what I said and report it to your master. I went easy on you today. I won't next time."

Conryu walked back to the girl, willed the library doors open, and led her through. Once they were safe inside he said, "If you know where your parents are, I can take you to them before we leave the country."

"My parents are dead. Shot for conceiving an abomination in God's eyes. I have no one and nowhere to go." She wiped tears from her eyes. "What will become of me?"

He offered her a gentle smile. "Whatever you want. I'll take you somewhere safe. And you won't be alone."

The library shifted at his command and the doors opened again. Two of the ninjas ushered a pair of girls through before vanishing. Conryu repeated the process with each group until he'd collected all the future wizards. Finally, he retrieved Kai and Kanna from the now-calm sky above the first village.

"How are the troops?" Conryu asked.

"No injuries on our side and no deaths on theirs," Kanna said. "Before I forget, here's the second crystal."

"Excellent." Conryu took the stone. It looked exactly like the one in his pocket. "Remember how I said you guys needed to find a new home? I'm going to take you to a potential location. You don't mind the cold, do you?"

Kanna raised an eyebrow drawing a grin from Conryu. He willed the library to the Land of the Night Princes. If anyone could understand what the girls had been through, it would be the former White Witches. And no one would dare threaten them in a land surrounded by vampires.

---

Conryu and Kai stepped out of the library an hour after dark. An abandoned city sprawled in every direction. The buildings tended to be less than thirty stories and the streets had weeds growing up out of holes in the pavement. He wanted to check with Lord Talon before he brought thirty-odd girls into his country. Not that he figured the vampire lord would object, but it was rude to just assume.

Only the building directly in front of them had lights in a few of the windows. Not much had changed from the last time they visited. That was just as well since in Conryu's experience, things seldom changed for the better.

At least it was still warm. The Land of the Night Princes was not pleasant in the winter. He looked up at the stars. This was one of the best places to study the sky. The sparse population assured a minimum of light pollution.

"Chosen."

"I sense them too. Relax, we're on good terms with everyone." Of course, relaxing when surrounded by half a dozen vampires, friends or not, was easier said than done.

"Conryu?" A beautiful, dark-haired vampire appeared as though out of nowhere. It was Anya's mother, Sasha. She wore a stunning, midnight-blue dress slit up to the hip and her lips seemed especially red against her pale skin. "What a nice surprise. Does Lord Talon know you were coming?"

"No, it was sort of a spur of the moment decision. It's good to see you again, Sasha."

"You as well. Talon is in the east patrolling the border. We've had no incursions since the Dragon Emperor's death, but he takes nothing for granted. One of the others is going to fetch him. Would you like to come in? Anya will be thrilled to see you."

"Thank you." They followed Sasha into the apartment building, through the empty lobby, and to the stairs. "We still haven't gotten the elevators working, I'm afraid."

"How are the former White Witches settling in?"

"Very well. The winter was a long one for them, but we've found work for everyone. Thankfully they each had a skill of some sort outside of magic."

"Speaking of magic, has anyone reconsidered about resuming their life as a wizard?" Conryu asked.

"Not that they've mentioned to me. Anya has kept up with her practice and has even devised a couple minor spells of her own." She sounded so proud Conryu couldn't help smiling. Sasha opened a door to the third floor. "Here we are."

In the hall a pair of middle-aged women were chatting outside their apartment doors. Conryu didn't remember their names, but they knew him and waved. He smiled and returned the gesture. Sasha led the way to the last apartment on the left. It was a small unit, just a living room with a coffin in place of a couch and two chairs. Beyond that was a kitchenette and two doors that he assumed led to a bedroom and bathroom. All very ordinary, if you didn't count the coffin.

"Kiska! We have company."

The bedroom door opened and there stood one of the most beautiful women he'd ever met. Anya's blond hair had grown down past her waist. She wore comfortable lounge pants and a tank top cut off above her belly button. Calling her stunning would be a vast understatement.

"Conryu." Anya ran over and hugged him.

Years of training allowed him to control his reaction when she pressed herself against his chest. Still, just as well Maria wasn't here. The two women had come to an understanding but seeing her like this might be pushing his luck.

"Anya," he said when she finally let go. "Your mother tells me you've been keeping up with your magical training."

"Just simple stuff. What brings you by?"

"I need a favor. If you don't mind, I'll wait until Lord Talon arrives, so I don't have to explain twice."

"Sure, have a seat." Anya went to the kitchenette. "Want some coffee?"

"No, thanks." He settled into one of the chairs and sighed. It had been a long couple of days and the soft leather felt wonderful. "What does he have you guys doing?"

"Cleaning and restoration mostly," Anya said.

"Lord Talon hopes to bring this city back to life," Sasha said. "It will take time to convince more humans to move here, but if they wish to, he wants to have places for them to stay."

A tall, dark figure materialized in the middle of the living room. Talon looked exactly as Conryu remembered. Tall, handsome, and pale, dressed in all black, he was the very definition of a vampire.

"My ears are burning. Have you been discussing me?"

Conryu stood and they shook hands. "Nothing scandalous I promise."

Talon laughed. "I'm sure. What brings you here, my friend?"

"I need help." Conryu explained about rescuing the girls. "I couldn't think of a safer place for them. It's a big ask I know, but can they stay here, at least for a little while?"

"Of course. As you can see, we have plenty of room. I may christen this building a shelter for abused wizards if you keep bringing them to me."

Conryu smiled, but it was tinged with sadness. Far too many wizards were abused in this world and he couldn't save them all, no matter how powerful he was.

"Where would you like me to bring them?" Conryu asked. "A living room with a coffin might be a little unnerving to start."

"Follow me. Anya, would you join us and greet our new guests?"

"Yes, my lord. Let me throw on a robe." Anya ducked into her room and closed the door.

Conryu reached into his pocket and pulled out one of the crystals. "Ever seen one of these?"

Talon took the crystal and looked it all over. "It's not a diamond. What is it?"

"It's a crystal and the cultists were using it to determine the magic potential of girls as young as thirteen. It's not magical. At least not in any way I can detect."

"A mystery indeed." Talon handed it back to him. "I'm sorry I can't be of more help."

"Taking in the girls is a huge help. Sasha mentioned you had to patrol the border. I think I can help with that."

Talon raised a perfectly shaped eyebrow. "Oh?"

"My bodyguards need a new home. I thought maybe they

could watch the border in exchange for a remote spot to set up a new village."

He glanced at Kai who was still standing silently beside him. "More like her?"

"Yeah, about seventy. Their old village has been compromised and is no longer safe."

"I know just the place. And yes, their help would be most welcome."

"I'm all set." Anya had swapped her pajamas for a brown earth magic user's robe.

They went to an empty apartment and Conryu opened the library. It was going to be a long night, but at least the girls would be safe.

---

Talon's perfect place for Kanna and the other ninjas turned out to be an abandoned monastery in the mountains. The stone of the main structure had seen its share of bad weather, but otherwise it appeared solid enough to Conryu. If it became necessary, he could make any modifications they needed with earth magic. There were cells enough for everyone and a large courtyard where they could train.

With the sun coming up, the mountains were beautiful. Their island was beautiful in its own way, but this was more his style. Conryu stifled a yawn. He'd been up all night reassuring the girls that they wouldn't end up as undead servants or just snacks for the vampires. Talon and his people had a terrible reputation, especially in the cult's territory. You'd think that would be enough to convince them given how the priests treated wizards.

Anya had done more than he had to calm their nerves. She was good with frightened girls. Probably having been a frightened girl running for her life once upon a time made her more understanding. At any rate they were settled for now and that was enough for him.

Leaving Kanna to get used to her new home, Conryu and Kai stepped into the border of Hell. As always Cerberus was waiting for him with a wagging tail.

"Will we not travel through the library?" Kai asked.

"We will, but first I need to talk to someone else about those crystals. Talon had never seen anything like them which, given his age, is remarkable. Prime didn't recognize them either. Dark Lady!" Conryu's summons was carried on winds of dark magic deeper into Hell. His demonic agent shouldn't take long to respond. "If she doesn't know what it is, then I'll really be worried."

A short time later, a crimson light resolved into the voluptuous figure of the Dark Lady. She was, as was her habit, dressed like a dominatrix in black leather. She was also wearing the thigh-high leather boots he'd gotten her for Christmas. Her bat wings were open and her hair was blown back in the breeze of her flight.

Conryu sighed. He had far more beautiful women in his life than was prudent. Not that he would trade any of them for anything.

The Dark Lady stopped, snapped her wings closed behind her, and bowed so low her breasts nearly escaped her bodice. She straightened and offered a smile that would have made most men weak in the knees. "Master. How may I be of service?"

He took out a crystal. "Ever seen one of these? It's used to detect magic potential in girls far younger than anything we have."

She looked anywhere but at the crystal. If he hadn't seen it with his own eyes, he wouldn't have believed it possible, but she actually looked uncomfortable.

"I can't say, Master."

"Does that mean you don't know?"

"It is forbidden by the Reaper's law. If you'd shown that crystal to anyone else in Hell, they likely would have killed you."

Prime snorted and Conryu raised an eyebrow.

"Or tried to," she amended. "I am sorry, Master. Is there something I can do to make it up to you?"

That was more like the Dark Lady he knew. "There is, actually."

Her eyes widened and she licked her lips.

"Not that. Do you know Jemma St. Simon's demonic agent?"

"No, but I can find them. Why?"

"I want to arrange a meeting, not in London. There's a bar in Tokyo called The Blowfish. Tell her to meet me there in two days at nine local time. Okay?"

"The Blowfish in Tokyo at nine local time in two days. No problem." The Dark Lady turned to leave then spun back. "Be careful, Master. Whatever danger you believe you're in, double it."

With that last warning she took off. Cerberus whined and Conryu offered a reassuring pat to his flank. Whatever the crystal was, it really scared the Dark Lady and there wasn't much capable of doing that.

"Do you not trust Jemma?" Kai asked. "I thought you two had a good working relationship."

"We're happy to use each other for our own purposes," Conryu said. "But she always has the best interests of her country in mind. If that coincides with my best interests then great, but if it doesn't you can guess who'll get the short end of the stick. She sent me after something that scares the Dark Lady and I'm not sure if she did it knowingly or otherwise. Until I figure out her game, I'm taking precautions."

"So what now?" Kai asked.

Conryu rubbed his tired eyes. "What time would you say it is at the Academy right now?"

Kai cocked her head as she thought. "Eight, nine o'clock maybe."

"I need you to take a message to Maria. Have her meet me in the library and tell her to bring Dean Blane with her."

# CHAPTER 6

Maria sat on her bed, propped up by four pillows. It was just after nine and her roommate was already snoring softly. She had the right idea, but Maria had to finish the book she was reading. It was a text discussing the theory of light magic healing in a way she'd never considered. And given how much time she spent thinking about stuff like that, it was saying something.

She'd only been back to school for a few days and she already missed Conryu terribly. She sighed and marked her page. Her train of thought had run off the rails. Might as well go to sleep and try again in the morning before first period.

A faint chill filled the air before a hand clamped over her mouth. "I didn't wish you to call out," Kai whispered in her ear.

The hand eased and Maria asked, "Is Conryu okay?"

"He's fine and waiting for you in the library. A mystery has come up and he needs help unraveling it. He also requested that you bring Dean Blane with you."

If Conryu wanted to involve the dean, it must be serious. Maria slipped out of bed and tossed her white robe over her pajamas. Dean Blane stayed in rooms on the ground floor at the rear of the dorm. Hopefully she wasn't still in her office.

"I'm ready," Maria said, but Kai was already gone. "Ninjas."

She glanced at her roommate, but the girl hadn't even stirred. Thank goodness for heavy sleepers.

The halls were empty as she made her way downstairs to the lobby. Maria didn't dare summon a light, so she enhanced her vision instead. The stairs and furniture appeared in clear black and white. A partially hidden door led to the dean's rooms. It wasn't locked so Maria went down a short hall to another closed door.

She knocked and half a minute later the door opened revealing the youthful form of Dean Blane. She looked about twelve thanks to transformation magic and her pink pajamas did nothing to undercut the impression. Dean Blane brushed her dark hair aside and rubbed her eyes.

"Maria? What on earth are you doing here at this time of night?"

Maria smiled. "What else? Conryu's here and he needs to see us."

"What's that boy gotten himself into now?" Dean Blane cocked her head. "And why can't I sense him?"

"Kai said he was waiting in the library. I assumed she meant our library, but maybe she meant his. Conryu wouldn't want to announce the fact that he was here to the entire staff."

"Good point." Dean Blane snapped her fingers and her slippers transformed into comfortable shoes. "Well, let's go see what he wants."

They crossed the campus surrounded by an invisibility spell so they wouldn't draw the eye of anyone staring out a window. Dean Blane asked no questions which was just as well since Maria knew only a little more than she did.

The library was dark and silent at this time of night. A large table where once upon a time she caught Conryu trying to research elf artifacts sat empty. Maria was just starting to wonder if Conryu had been playing a prank on them when a door appeared out of nowhere. It opened and there he was waiting for them in jeans, a t-shirt, and scuffed biker boots. The only thing that separated him from the standard biker was the glowing staff in his right hand.

"Thanks for meeting me. Come on in." He stepped aside so Maria and Dean Blane could enter. "I think I've gotten mixed up in a mess."

"What else is new?" Maria said. "I thought you were going to fix bikes and stay out of trouble."

"That was the plan, but Jemma needed my help."

"Jemma's involved?" Dean Blane asked. "If this is an official matter involving the Kingdom of the Isles I may have to let someone know."

"It's not," Conryu said. "She came to me because her government couldn't, or at least felt like they couldn't, get involved directly."

He filled them in on the details and when they were caught up took a crystal out of his pocket. "The Dark Lady knows what it is but is forbidden to speak by the Reaper's decree. Jemma claimed not to know what the cultists were using, but I'm not sure if I trust her."

Dean Blane took the crystal and muttered a spell. She frowned and cast another, this time in a louder, more strident tone. Her frown deepened and she looked up at him. "I've never encountered anything like this and I've studied the artifacts in the national archive. You may very well have discovered an entirely new sort of magic. Assuming it is magic."

"So you can't tell me anything about it?" he asked.

She shook her head. "Not yet. Can I keep this? I'd like to

study it closer, maybe have some of the other teachers take a look as well."

"Sure, go ahead. I'm going to ask a few of Kai's associates to keep an eye on the Academy. After the incident with the dragons, I'll feel better knowing someone is here to help if you guys need it."

"Sure, sure." Dean Blane was focused on the crystal again, having seemingly forgotten he was even there.

"How are the girls you rescued?" Maria asked.

"Safe but shaken. I mean, who moves into an empty city in a nation of vampires and finds it safer than home? Talk about screwed up. Anya and the White Witches will get them settled in and Lord Talon will protect them. I hate to leave so soon, but I need to sleep before I meet with Jemma. If it's a setup I want to be at my best."

Maria shook her head. "I can't believe she'd betray you after everything you've done for the Kingdom. Still, I'm glad you're taking precautions. Be careful."

She kissed him and they embraced. Conryu sighed and let her and Dean Blane out of the library then let Kai in. Why did his life have to be so bloody complicated?

🜚

The village square looked to Merik like a tornado had touched down and shredded the grass in a near perfect circle. He'd never seen anything like it. Magic had to have been involved. It was impossible to think that the fanatics could go on killing potential wizards forever without bringing down some sort of retribution on their heads. At the very least, the wizard's outburst should have helped smooth his path to gaining the bishop's help.

None of the locals appeared willing to enter the circle of

damage. They stared at Merik as he looked around as though expecting his flesh to start melting at any moment. The villagers probably thought the earth cursed now that magic had touched it. That was the sort of foolish notion the priests taught their followers. Some of them were even stupid enough to believe it.

Merik shrugged and marched out of the square. He'd seen a collection of tents on his way into town. That was where he'd find his contact.

His original plan had been to simply send another dupe to Stonehenge to activate the pillar, but now that he'd had time to consider his options, it was clear that his original plan had little hope of success. However, where a single errand boy might fail, a squad of armed fanatics might have better luck.

He would have altered his plans in the first place, but he'd never considered the possibility that the wizard assassin would be waiting. A foolish oversight. She had to have known where the key to Atlantis's return was hidden. Oh well. Merik was still learning to think strategically and not like a traveling salesman.

Outside the tents, a pair of heavily muscled thugs dressed in priestly black complete with white collars stood with their arms crossed outside the largest white canvas tent. They stared hard at Merik as he approached. A less determined man might have turned aside under the glare of those harsh eyes.

The guard on the right raised his hand palm out. "The bishop is indisposed. Get lost."

"Tell the bishop that Merik is here to see him. Considering your recent encounter, I assure you he'll want to speak with me."

The lead guard nodded toward the tent flap and his companion ducked inside. Merik couldn't make out what the voices were saying, but a minute later the guard returned and held the flap open. "He will see you."

Merik ducked into the cool, dim interior. The bishop sat on one of two camp stools behind a folding desk. He wore a formal white cassock and gold cross even in the privacy of his tent. The tent was as spare as anything Merik had ever seen. The only nod to rank was the fact that he apparently didn't have to share his lodgings. Merik had never cared for camping as a boy and he liked it even less as a grown man. Unfortunately, since beginning his new life as a Child of Atlantis he'd found himself in primitive surroundings more often than he'd prefer.

The bishop looked up from whatever he was working on. "Merik. I assumed we wouldn't see you again after you gifted us with those remarkable crystals. They worked wonderfully by the way. At least until that goddamned wizard arrived and stole them. The man came at us like Satan himself. Dare I hope you've come with replacements?"

"No. There are no replacements outside of Atlantis. In fact, that is what brings me to you. I have met greater resistance in my quest than I anticipated. I need reinforcements. A single wizard stands between me and the completion of my mission. If you could loan me some soldiers to deal with her, I'm sure the people of Atlantis would be very grateful. In fact, there are few more sympathetic to the cause of killing wizards. It was the wizards that nearly wiped Atlantis off the map forever after all."

The bishop stroked his chin whiskers. "It is becoming clear to me that if we are to complete God's holy mission, we will need allies. If the Atlanteans were to convert to the worship of the True Face of God, I'm certain His Grace would permit me to lend whatever aid you needed."

*Promise the fool whatever you must. Once we're free it won't matter.*

"I don't believe your church existed before the fall of Atlantis," Merik said. "But once you explain your beliefs to them, I'm certain the True Face of God will be very popular."

The bishop's smile was so arrogant Merik wanted to punch his face in. "Then for our future brothers and sisters in God, my men and I will join you in your noble quest."

Merik forced himself to bow. "Thank you very much, your eminence."

"Where does our crusade take us?"

"Stonehenge."

---

Tokyo made Sentinel City look like a backwater village. It sprawled over nearly a third of the island of Honshu and its towering skyscrapers cast the lower reaches of the city in perpetual twilight. The noise from millions of cars filled the air along with the fumes from their exhaust. It was like home, but different.

The shadows shrouding the streets suited Conryu fine. He wasn't looking to draw attention, which was why he chose a city he'd never visited for this meeting. The odds of running into someone he knew were so small as to be nonexistent. It was also why he had Prime hidden in a shoulder bag.

Not that any of the fifty million residents he'd encountered showed the least interest in him as he made his way through the throngs to the working-class district which was home to The Blowfish. He'd exited the library half a mile from his rendezvous in the hopes of spotting an ambush.

Not that he really expected one. He was being overly

cautious, but that weird crystal that was magic but didn't read as magic had him spooked. The Dark Lady's reaction to it had done nothing to ease his nerves. Hopefully Maria and Dean Blane would have some answers for him next time he checked in.

He probably should have done a quick search to make sure The Blowfish was still open since his father's stories were twenty years old. The name had just popped into his head and he blurted it out. His Japanese was rusty, but good enough to let him find the street he wanted.

Relief flooded through him when he spotted a round, spiky fish drawn in flickering neon over the entrance to a hole-in-the-wall bar. Looked like it was still open.

Conryu checked his phone. He was ten minutes early. He ducked through the doorway and looked over the tiny bar. There were only six tables and eight stools. No servers patrolled the floor. A single wrinkled woman stood behind the bar, her eyes half closed as she watched the lone customer, an equally ancient man, nurse his beer.

He crossed the room, offered his best smile, and said, "Two beers, Obasan."

Her wrinkles nearly swallowed her face when she smiled. "Your accent is appalling, young man." She spoke English with only a faint accent.

"I'm out of practice. My dad was from the Empire. He came here once with a friend of his back in the day. Figured I'd check it out while I was in town."

She pulled two bottles of frosty beer out from under the counter and handed them to him. "Meeting someone?"

"Yeah, she should be along soon. How much?"

"Do you have Imperial yen?"

Conryu winced. "All I've got are Kingdom pounds."

She shrugged. "A five will do it."

He dug the bill out of his wallet and slid it across the bar to her. "Thanks."

Conryu grabbed a corner table that gave him a clear view of the entrance. If Jemma was following standard protocol, she should arrive early to have a look around. He'd actually expected to find her waiting.

He popped the cap and took a sip of the beer. How did people drink that stuff on a regular basis? He'd tried it once before in high school at a party with Jonny and couldn't get over the bitter taste. Thankfully, Jemma stepped through the entrance before he had to try another swallow. She was dressed in civilian clothes, red sundress, black shoes, and a leather purse. She actually looked like a regular tourist.

She spotted him at once and stalked over, her face like a thundercloud. Jemma dropped into the chair opposite him. Before she could speak, Conryu willed a wind barrier in place to stop their voices from reaching the rest of the bar.

"What's the big idea dragging me all the way here?" Jemma asked. "Our spies said you rescued a bunch of the girls. Did you find what they were using to determine who to kill?"

Jemma seemed sincere. Maybe he'd read too much into her sending him on this job.

"Here." Conryu slid the clear crystal across the table to her. "This is why I was being so careful. It's like no magic I've ever encountered. I did a little digging and my contacts either don't know what it is, or they aren't able to talk about it."

Her palm covered the crystal and she concentrated. After a minute of silence, she said, "I see what you mean. Something like this, if word got out, could change the world. Still, you could have brought it to me in London."

"I wasn't sure you weren't setting me up. Plus, the crystal itself rattled me. What are you going to do with it?"

"Give it to the research department, see what they can

make of it. What did you mean when you said your contacts couldn't talk about the crystal?"

Conryu told her about the Dark Lady. "The demons at least know what it is. I suspect the other spirits do as well and I further suspect they'll have been banned from speaking about it by their various masters. Whatever this thing is, they very badly want to keep it a secret."

"Does that scare you as much as it does me?"

"Yeah, it scares the hell out of me."

## CHAPTER 7

Jonny Salazar stood at ease, hands clasped behind his back, outside the commander's office. The door was shut and the small waiting room empty. There weren't even chairs. Having to stand while you waited was probably part of the punishment when you were called to the office. But as far as he knew, he hadn't done anything wrong.

He hadn't encountered any more zombies since those two the other day. Turned out, undead washing up on the beach happened far less often than he'd thought. The other teams reported only one other incident over the base's entire sector. Since he hadn't done anything but walk up and down the water's edge, Jonny couldn't imagine why his commanding officer had called him in, especially without his trainer.

There was a sound beyond the door and a moment later it opened. Major Evans, the base commander, waved him in. Jonny stepped inside and the major stepped out, closing the door behind him. Seated behind the painfully neat desk was an older man in a green uniform, his chest covered with about ten pounds of medals. Two gold stars shone on his collar.

Bloody hell, what did a general want with him?

Jonny saluted. "Reporting as ordered, sir."

"At ease, Private. I imagine you're curious why you're here."

"Yes, sir."

"Would it surprise you to learn it's because of your friend the wizard?"

Jonny's heart skipped a beat. "Conryu? Is he okay?"

"He's fine as far as we know. Apparently, he's attacked the True Face of God's nation and kidnapped over thirty of their citizens. Their archbishop has complained to the joint Alliance command as well as to the president directly. They blame us since he is still technically an Alliance citizen."

"That doesn't seem like something Conryu would do, sir. Not without an excellent reason anyway."

"His reasons might be excellent, or they might be lousy. It doesn't matter. We can't have one of our citizens, even one that no longer lives here, invading sovereign nations. It makes us look either weak or belligerent. At the moment the president wishes to be seen as neither. We need to bring him in."

Jonny didn't like where this was going. If the army got into a fight with Conryu, things would get ugly in a hurry.

"I'm not sure that's a good idea, sir."

"I'm not asking your opinion, Private. We know you have some way of contacting him. Your task is to call him in. Say whatever you have to. Once Conryu shows up, we have a team ready to capture him. Our researchers have found a way to negate his magic."

"You're asking me to lure my best friend, a man I owe my life to several times over, into a trap?"

"I'm not asking you to do anything." The general stood. Despite his age he was still a bear of a man. "I'm telling you, that's what you're going to do. Why do you think you're here?"

Jonny cocked his head. "Sir?"

"You're in the most coveted posting in the military. It's not because of any minor heroics you may have performed during the recent crises. Your sole purpose is to provide a conduit to Conryu. He trusts you. There's no one else we could use to draw him in. You will contact him. You will tell him to meet you at a time and place of our choosing. Is that clear?"

"Perfectly, sir."

"Good. Take a seat. You won't be leaving my sight until the op is complete."

"When is it happening, sir?"

"Tonight. We're in the process of clearing the target area."

"When should I reach out?" Jonny asked.

"Now."

Jonny licked his lips and dug the rune stone Conryu had given him out of his pocket. The smooth stone was marked with three vertical lines crossed by two others at a forty-five-degree angle. It was about as big around as a quarter and half an inch thick.

He hesitated.

Should he do this?

Conryu would never set him up.

The general's stare never wavered. The truth, Jonny now understood, was that he really had no choice. He felt kind of bad for whoever they sent to try and capture Conryu. His best friend had a big heart, but little patience for any kind of foolishness.

"Any time now, Private."

Right. He took a deep breath and placed the stone to his temple. "Are you there, bro?"

There was nothing for a few seconds then, "Jonny, what's wrong? Are you in trouble?"

"We found something. Some weird magic thing. The army wizards don't know how to handle it. I thought maybe you could take a look. Can you meet me tonight after our guys finish and head back to the barracks?"

"Is it some sort of crystal?" Conryu asked.

"Yeah, a crystal. Can you check it out?"

"I'll be there. What time?"

"Ten local. I'll be waiting."

"Okay, I can home in on your stone so be sure and have it with you."

"I always have it with me. Thanks man, see you later." The connection severed and Jonny lowered the stone. "He's coming."

"Very good, Private." The general frowned. "Why did you mention a crystal?"

"He asked me if we found a crystal. I don't know why, but I figured if I agreed he'd be more apt to come."

"Yes, good thinking. You may have a future in military intelligence. Try to relax. You're going to have a busy night."

Sure, how often did he get to betray his oldest friend?

※

Jonny stood at an intersection near a construction site. The sun had set several hours ago leaving the area dark and silent. Local law enforcement had evacuated everyone under the pretense of a gas leak.

How many times had he heard that excuse in a movie or tv show? More times than he could remember, but apparently it worked in real life as well.

He checked his watch. Fifteen minutes before Conryu arrived. While he hadn't met the team that was supposed to capture his best friend, he assumed they were hidden nearby. This was going to be a nightmare. He didn't care what they thought they'd found, stopping Conryu, assuming he didn't want to be stopped, would be no simple task. In truth he doubted it was even possible.

No matter. He'd done his part. Now all he had to do was stand here and be the bait.

He glanced at his watch again. Five more minutes. Would he just step out of nowhere beside Jonny? No, more likely he'd arrive nearby and approach on foot so as not to give him a heart attack.

"Come on, bro, where are you?"

Jonny took a step to the right and fell into an endless white light.

When the sparkles vanished, he found himself floating among fluffy white clouds. In contrast to the heavenly surroundings, a scowling Conryu hovered directly in front of him. His knuckles were white on the shaft of his staff.

"Dude, the artifact. Why did—"

"Stop, please." Conryu blew out a long sigh. "How long have we known each other?"

Jonny stared for a moment, taken off guard by the question. "Like fifteen years."

"In that time, I've determined one thing for sure. You are the worst liar I've ever met. I kept listening through the rune stone after you took it away from your head."

Jonny winced. "I didn't have a choice. When a general gives an order, privates obey, no questions asked."

"Just following orders. That's going to be your excuse? What did the military tell you to convince you to set me up?"

"That you invaded a country and kidnapped a bunch of citizens. That's bullshit though right?"

"What it is, is a very misleading description of what happened. I didn't kidnap anyone. I rescued some girls that were going to be burned at the stake for the crime of being born potential wizards. Burned alive, Jonny. Can you imagine a worse way to die? They were only thirteen. What would your commanders have me do, let them die? Let thirty-plus innocent girls burn to death because it's not convenient politics?"

"It's complicated." That sounded lamer out loud than it had in his head.

"No, it isn't. Either you're in favor of letting people burn alive or you're not. And, assuming you're against it, if you have the power to do something about it, then stepping aside isn't an option. I chose to help those girls and I'd do it again. If the government you serve sees things differently, you might want to give serious thought about finding another career."

Jonny had never heard his friend this angry. Conryu was usually the most laid-back guy he knew. "What happens now?"

Conryu snapped his fingers and Jonny's rune stone appeared in his hand. "I can't trust you with this anymore. Not as long as you're willing to follow the orders of men that will condemn me for saving the lives of innocents. You want to ditch the uniform and come with me; we'll talk. Otherwise, I'll drop you somewhere near your base."

Jonny wanted to pull his hair out. He shouldn't have been surprised. Hell, he knew Conryu was going to be pissed and he followed his orders anyway. Not that he'd had much of a choice considering he was on a base surrounded by soldiers who would have thrown him in the brig without a second thought had he refused.

He had a chance to walk away now, but if he did, he might never be able to see his family again. Or worse, the government might retaliate against them somehow. He was pretty sure the only reason they left Conryu's mom alone was because they knew what he might do if they messed with her. No one was afraid of Jonny Salazar.

"Sorry, dude. The army is a little like the mafia. You can't just walk away without consequences."

"Too bad, but I understand. Good luck." Conryu held out his hand and Jonny shook it. The next thing he knew they were standing on the beach about three miles from the base. "It's a bit of a walk, but I'm sure you'll manage."

With that parting thought, Conryu vanished.

Jonny silently cursed General No Name for screwing up the best friendship he'd ever had. The worst part was he'd probably still end up in the brig. Some general wasn't going to accept responsibility for Conryu getting away. They'd blame the private, give him thirty days or something, and move on to plotting some other way to make trouble for Conryu. Because whatever else, Jonny had no doubt the powers that be weren't about to let his friend off the hook just because this scheme failed.

He trudged off the sand and down a nearby sidewalk. Salsa music blared from one of the many dance clubs lining the street. For once in his life, Jonny didn't want to party, he just wanted to hit the rack and get some sleep. The stress of the past few hours had left him exhausted.

It took half an hour for him to reach the front gate at the weary pace he set. Part of him wasn't at all anxious to finish the trip. At the guardhouse two soldiers armed with rifles said, "Halt and identify yourself."

"Private Salazar. I've been on a special mission for the general."

"What general?" one of the guards asked.

So the big boss hadn't let anyone know he was there. Terrific, one more screw-up on Jonny's record.

"Corporal, he's on the list." The second guard had fetched a clipboard from the shack and was studying the second sheet. "We're supposed to alert command if he shows up."

The corporal gave Jonny an appraising look. Probably

wondering if he should raise his weapon or not. Given that Jonny was unarmed it would be overkill.

"Can I wait in my bunk?" Jonny asked.

"You'll wait right where you are," the corporal said. His partner was already on the phone with the base commander. Jonny would be facing the music soon enough.

Soon enough came three minutes later when a camo jeep squealed to a stop just beyond the gate. Two MPs leapt out and waved Jonny in. The gate went up and he was hustled into the back seat before they went squealing into the dark. The MPs never said a word during the short drive to the command building.

Just outside the door the driver finally spoke. "He's waiting for you in the commander's office."

Jonny didn't need to be told who. He hopped out of the jeep, and quick stepped through the empty building to the office at the rear. The door was open and the general sat behind the office desk looking exactly like Jonny left him.

"Close the door behind you," the general said.

Jonny obeyed and said, "I'm sorry, sir. I had no idea Conryu would just open a portal under my feet like that."

"The target was clearly on guard. I don't blame you. I heard every word you said and you clearly didn't warn him. When it comes to these sorts of operations, you have to accept that you might not succeed on the first try. It's why I hate magic. All the best plans mean nothing when the rules of nature don't apply."

The tightness flowed out of Jonny's shoulders and chest. "What happens now, sir?"

"What did he tell you?" the general asked.

"Conryu? He explained why he did what he did. Said he didn't kidnap anyone. He offered to take me with him and when I declined, he took my rune stone so if I need magical help I'm out of luck. After that he dumped me on the beach and vanished."

"That's it?"

"Yes, sir."

"Why didn't you take him up on his offer?"

"I made a commitment to the army and I don't break my word lightly." Not the whole truth, but Jonny figured it was close enough.

"Very well, Private. You will resume your duties in the morning. Dismissed."

Jonny saluted, turned on his heel, and marched out. Somehow, he'd made it through without losing his position. Was it worth losing his best friend? He didn't know yet.

CHAPTER 8

Kai stood on a rooftop overlooking the spot where Conryu was supposed to meet his friend. At his request, she'd arrived well before the meeting was supposed to take place. He was cautious about this rendezvous, a mindset that she wholly approved of. Though reluctant to leave his side, she had come to understand that what the Chosen needed was less a bodyguard than an assistant. For all his immense power, he couldn't be everywhere at once. Her job tonight was to be his eyes while he spoke to his friend.

She frowned and adjusted her sword. In the dark and silent section of the city, the lights of an approaching vehicle stood out like signal flares. They intended to be punctual at least. Early in fact. To set a trap? Conryu thought so. He read something in his friend's voice when they spoke, something he didn't like.

The vehicle stopped and Jonny got out. She recognized his dark complexion and cocky stance even from a distance. Kai hadn't interacted with him directly many times, but she'd watched him with Conryu enough to know him when she saw him. The truck took off, leaving him at the intersection, alone.

Maybe it wasn't a trap after all.

Kai stepped into the borderland and emerged a second later on a different rooftop. A hint of movement in one of the alleys near the intersection caught her eye. She took a small pair of binoculars out of her belt pouch and looked closer. A single figure in dark camouflage and body armor, a rifle slung across his back and the hilt of a knife jutting up at his hip, inched closer to where Jonny waited. The soldier didn't get too close.

Wise of him. A wizard of Conryu's power would have no trouble sensing someone's life force if they got careless.

No way did the military send a single man to try and capture the strongest wizard in the world. There had to be more.

Kai shifted to a third roof and looked around again. Now that she knew what to watch out for, she spotted the second soldier almost immediately. The moment she did her frown deepened.

He was standing directly under her previous perch. She should have sensed his presence at once from that distance. Kai in no way overestimated her abilities, but if there was one thing she was better than Conryu at, it was stealth and locating targets that believed they were hidden. She'd trained her entire life as an assassin. To miss something so obvious rankled her pride.

Her internal clock said she only had five minutes left. Should be time enough to sort out this little mystery.

Another quick step through Hell brought her to a spot directly above the first man she spotted. Kai knew he was directly below her; if she looked over the edge of the roof, she could've dropped a dagger on his head. Which might not be a terrible idea if he was a threat to Conryu, but she couldn't sense his life force. Something was shielding him. A new stealth magic of some kind perhaps.

At any rate Conryu was clearly wise to have taken precautions. Kai used her remaining time to search the rest of the area around Jonny. She found a third man only half a minute before the appointed time. They clearly knew what they were doing, but they were too far away to stop Conryu.

Shifting her gaze to the intersection, Kai counted down the seconds.

At the appointed moment, a white portal appeared directly under Jonny's feet. He vanished and the portal closed behind him. The look on his face would have brought the grin she loved so much to Conryu's face. However she was focused on the soldiers' reaction.

The one she was watching snapped his head up and touched something at his throat. His lips moved but she couldn't make out what he was mumbling. A moment later he ran toward the intersection and met his two companions. At least she hadn't missed anyone. That would have been too embarrassing.

They had a conference and a few minutes later the truck that delivered Jonny pulled up and collected them. Kai vanished into Hell and followed the truck through the city directly back to the nearest military base. They were waved through and she followed.

Or at least she tried to. At the fence, she slammed face first into an invisible barrier that extended all the way into Hell. If she was a gambling woman, she would have put money on the ward blocking magical access from all the elemental realms. The precaution didn't really surprise her. They couldn't very well have spies wandering their base, invisible in another reality.

Kai rose into the hellish sky and watched the truck make its way to a long building that resembled a huge tube cut in half with walls installed on either end. The soldiers got out and went inside.

That was all she needed to see.

A quick survey of the base perimeter revealed a blind spot in their defenses. Kai emerged from Hell and drew her sword. It crackled with dark energy. The lightest touch allowed her to cut a circle out of the steel mesh and slip inside the base. She had an excellent sense of direction and began working her way toward the building where she last saw the soldiers. The big sodium lights created deep pools of shadow.

Kai moved from one to the next, her black uniform making her nearly invisible. A pair of soldiers approached from her left.

She darted to a dark spot at the rear of a long building that stank of gas and oil. Crouching in the darkness, she held her breath and waited for them to pass.

Being unable to enter Hell at will left her feeling exposed. It was exciting and nerve-wracking at the same time. She hadn't felt the flutter of fear in her stomach in far too long. This was what she was trained for. For a time, she'd wondered if she'd ever get to use the skills she'd mastered before being selected as Conryu's protector.

The two men walked past less than ten feet from Kai's hiding place. They never even looked her way.

When they'd gone she let out a long breath. That had been close.

With the area clear she set out again. Five minutes and two close encounters later she reached the building the soldiers entered. She pressed her ear to the door and heard muffled voices.

Her sword made a two-inch hole a foot off the ground. She lay down and pressed her ear to it.

"Who cares if the crystal can stop magic!" someone shouted. "The range is so short we couldn't prevent the portal from opening. The target never even showed up."

"Calm down, Sergeant," a cool voice said. "We knew the capture of Conryu Koda wasn't going to be a simple task. The failure of our first effort, while disappointing, is not unexpected. Plan B is already in the works. If he won't come to us, we'll go to him."

Kai shifted so she could look through the opening. Three muscular men in dark uniforms faced a fourth, older man in green. He wore dozens of medals on his chest. Kai knew little about the military's ranking system, but anyone with that many ribbons on their chest had to be in charge.

The man in green held up a gray crystal suspended from a silver chain. "This is the equalizer, gentlemen. Once our R&D people figure out how to mass-produce these, we'll never have to fear a wizard again."

"If they figure it out," one of the soldiers said. "Rumor is the eggheads haven't even created one crystal of their own."

"It's been less than a year since we found the originals. Given enough time they will succeed."

Kai sensed someone approaching.

She scrambled to her feet, but too slow.

A pair of patrolling soldiers rounded the building and spotted her.

"Hands up!" Both men raised their rifles.

Kai lunged at them, slicing through the barrels of their weapons and leaving them so much junk.

At full speed she ran toward the fence, stealth forgotten.

A bullet pinged off the pavement six inches from her left foot.

She spotted the shooter in one of the lookout towers.

Without a ranged weapon her only option was to run a

random path and hope for the best. Behind her voices were raised and another bullet whizzed past her head.

The fence was in sight now.

She put on a final burst of speed and slashed it apart.

A sharp pain stabbed her side before Hell's welcoming darkness swallowed her up.

🜍

Merik and the fanatics worked their way through the trees surrounding Stonehenge. The moon was bright overhead, providing just enough light to see. At least, Merik could see with his enhanced senses. The priests were using night-vision goggles. Each man, including the bishop, carried an automatic rifle, grenades, knives, and enough ammo to invade London, again.

Crossing the Channel had proven remarkably simple. Considering all the trouble the Kingdom of the Isles had had over the past year, you'd think they'd have taken extra precautions to avoid anyone sneaking in. Maybe with the reconstruction they hadn't had time to raise the wards. Merik neither knew nor cared. Their carelessness made a difficult job at least a little easier.

They'd beached their boat on a narrow patch of sand that, from the looks of it, no one had visited in ages and set out at a quick march inland. No one spoke as they slipped through the forest. That combined with the way they handled their weapons led Merik to suspect they were priests in name only. Divine mercenaries was more like it. Not that it mattered. As long as they got past the assassin, they could call themselves anything they wanted.

A tingle ran through him as they got closer to the Lemurian wards that prevented him from approaching the standing stones. When that happened he'd have to stop and put his trust in his allies. It had taken all his will to place the crystal in the bishop's hands. If they lost it to the assassin, he didn't know what he'd do.

Merik repressed a shudder at the thought that these fanatics were his best hope of completing his mission. Clearly, he had gone wrong somewhere.

*The priest would tell you to have faith.*

Merik smiled to himself. The voice that spoke through his crystal had contacted him less often as he settled into his new life. Sometimes he found he missed the constant presence and encouragement. Other times he was happy to have his mind to himself. Tonight was a night for encouragement. Maybe he would finally meet her. It would be interesting to see if the owner of the voice looked anything like he imagined.

A jagged shard of pain stabbed him deep in his soul and brought an end to his musing. He had reached the border of the ward. "I can go no further."

The bishop nodded. "We know what to do. Dealing with wizards is our specialty."

He'd have a good deal more trouble dealing with this one than those girls who couldn't even use their magic. Merik contented himself with saying, "Good luck."

They vanished into the night, leaving Merik alone to await the outcome.

CHAPTER 9

Sienna floated, still and silent, at the edge of the realm of wind. There was nothing to see here, though she felt the spirits brushing up against her constantly. After her mother died and passed her duties as guardian on to Sienna, they had been her only steady companions.

She sighed. Someday, likely after the current crisis was dealt with, she would need to find a suitable mate. Serving as guardian wasn't something she could do forever and raising a replacement was part of her duty. She pushed the unpleasant thought out of her mind and focused.

After leaving the ridiculous professor behind, she had returned to her post watching over Stonehenge. She could feel the wards she set around the stones. It was only a matter of time before the Atlantean sent more agents to try and access the key to Atlantis. She would not let that happen. Even if it cost her life, she would find a way to prevent Atlantis returning. It was her duty as one of the few remaining direct decedents of Lemuria.

Though if she died, there would be no one to take her place.

Should that happen, the world would be exposed to a threat they didn't even know existed.

The activation of one of her wards snapped Sienna out of her mood. She waved a hand and murmured a spell to open a viewing window. A small force of heavily armed men was advancing toward the circle of stones. The Atlantean wasn't with them, but she could sense the key crystal. If she could only seize it and take the cursed thing somewhere secure, hunting down her target would be much easier.

But that was a big if. Sienna's magic wasn't especially powerful. Her gifts focused on movement and speed, not attack strength, which was why she carried the sword. Dealing with six armed men would be pushing it for her.

Win or lose, her duty was clear. She drew her sword, cast every enhancement spell she knew, and opened a portal.

The weight of the mortal realm grabbed her feet and dragged her to earth. The instant her feet touched she pushed off and rushed the nearest soldier.

To his credit, he snapped off three shots before her blade opened his throat.

The dead man's companions opened up on full auto.

Bullets whizzed past her head as Sienna sprinted across the clearing. Her speed was screwing up their aim, for the moment at least.

The man she sensed carrying the crystal was moving steadily toward the stones. She had to get to him.

One of the soldiers paused to reload.

The instant he did, Sienna sprinted at him.

His eyes went wide an instant before his head flew away.

She raced through the gap. The crystal bearer was only five paces away from the circle.

A bullet nicked her arm. Sienna forced the pain away and closed on her target.

"Watch out, Bishop!" one of the soldiers called.

The crystal bearer, Bishop she assumed, turned and fired his weapon.

She barely spun aside to avoid a chest full of lead.

His barrel followed her, forcing her further from the circle of stones.

Sienna shifted into the realm of wind and emerged an instant later directly in Bishop's path. He turned to face her in seeming slow motion.

The barrel of his rifle turned her sword aside, averting a killing blow.

She stepped closer, put her hand on his chest, and said, "Gust!"

The winds answered her spell's call. Bishop flew twenty feet, landed on his back, and skidded another ten feet before coming to a stop.

Before she could follow up a grenade arced in at her. She twirled her finger, sending the explosive flying aside. It exploded, nearly deafening her.

A fresh volley of bullets screamed all around her. Only the wind barrier she conjured earlier kept her skin intact. These soldiers knew their business. As they fired, the three men gathered around Bishop, helping him to his feet. Sienna ran behind one of the standing stones to give her shield a rest. The constant clatter of bullets made it hard to think.

"Surrender, wizard, and we'll let you live," one of the soldiers said.

Sienna didn't bother to reply. She would stop them or she would die trying. Her duty required nothing less.

"Be reasonable," he said. "I know you're wounded. Dying here won't do you any good."

Blood dripped down Sienna's left arm, but it was a minor wound, nothing that would lessen her combat effectiveness.

These people weren't fools. They had to know she wouldn't just give up. Why were they even trying?

She instantly shifted her awareness outward.

Too slow.

One of the soldiers stepped out from behind a stone and opened fire.

Sienna leapt aside, wind magic pushing further than her tired muscles could and cushioning her landing.

She barely had time to recover before a second grenade came soaring in. A gesture sent it flying back the way it had come.

Halfway between her and her enemies it exploded. A piece of shrapnel sent a wave of pain up her left leg. Across from her, one of the soldiers had jumped on top of Bishop, shielding him with his body. Now the leader of the group shoved his dead comrade aside and hurried toward the stones.

The surviving soldiers fired at Sienna, trying to pin her in place.

Blood loss made the world spin. She had maybe power enough for two more spells, before backlash set in. Once that happened, she would be helpless.

Bishop was only three paces from the circle. No time to worry about the consequences.

With the last of her magic, she cast a flying spell. She shot straight up then dove at Bishop.

Another bullet struck her good leg.

Her sword pierced the man through the back, knocking him through one of the arches and flat on his face.

Sienna ripped the blade free, spun, and opened the throat of a soldier rushing toward her. The last survivor raced toward Bishop.

She couldn't let him get the crystal.

Summoning her strength, a screaming headache already forming, she hurled her blade through the soldier's chest.

Sienna collapsed and curled into a ball of pain. She'd done it.

"You lose, wizard."

She rolled over in time to see a bloody Bishop drag himself into the center of the stones.

Sienna crawled toward him, but too slowly. A red crystal pillar appeared. Bishop reached up and placed the key stone into the empty divot just as she reached him.

A tremor ran through the earth and air then the pillar vanished. She reached out and touched the side of Bishop's neck.

No pulse.

She had defeated her foes but failed her mission.

Atlantis was returning.

---

Conryu paced through the sand as he waited for Kai. She was already an hour late and he was getting worried. They'd agreed to meet on a little island off the east coast that was outside the Alliance's magical detection zone after he let Jonny off. It wasn't much more than a ten-acre patch of stone and sand in the middle of the ocean.

He'd only stumbled across it by accident one day when the floating island drifted over it as he looked off one of the cliffs. They'd used it a couple times while running errands and it had seemed safe enough. Just like her mission. All he'd asked her to do was keep watch and see if Jonny really had set him up. Of course, his friend – strange that he still thought of Jonny as a friend – had admitted that was exactly what he'd done which made Kai's mission irrelevant.

"You fret too much, Master," Prime said. "This female is the most accomplished of your collection."

Conryu winced at Prime's description of his friends, but by now he was used to the scholomantic's lack of tact. "You're probably right, but I can't help worrying."

He'd give Kai ten more minutes before he went looking. She'd be annoyed if everything was okay, but he could live with that. If she was hurt and he did nothing… That, he couldn't live with.

After what felt like some of the longest minutes of his life, Conryu threw up his hands and opened a Hell portal. Cerberus was waiting as always on the other side. The demon dog whimpered. He probably sensed Conryu's anxiety.

"I need to find Kai," Conryu said. "Can you do that?"

Cerberus put his three heads into the air and sniffed. If Kai was anywhere in Hell, Cerberus would find her. At last the demon dog barked.

"Good boy." He leapt onto the beast's massive back. "Let's hunt!"

Cerberus took off like a shot. The feeling of rapid movement was all in Conryu's imagination since there were no landmarks to provide perspective in the endless darkness. Ahead of them, rapidly approaching, was a glowing speck surrounded by a trio of smaller specks.

The larger object quickly resolved into Kai's still body. The smaller trio were bat-winged imps flying around her, probably trying to work up nerve enough to get closer. Even from a distance Conryu could sense Kai's life force. It was weak, but there. Someone had hurt her, badly.

When he found out who, they'd wish they'd never been born.

A single bark from Cerberus sent the imps scattering.

Conryu gestured and Kai floated up beside him. She'd been shot in the side; her black uniform was soaked with blood.

"Take us somewhere safe, quickly."

Cerberus bolted again. Conryu couldn't use light magic to heal her in Hell. So much dark energy would render the spell useless. He didn't want to step out into the real world where he found her in case whoever shot her was waiting to finish the job.

He pressed hard against the wound. "Hang on, Kai."

A few seconds later Cerberus stopped and barked. Conryu didn't even bother with a viewing window, he just opened a portal and flew through it with Kai. They were in a field in the middle of nowhere. He laid her in the grass and sent healing energy through her body. The bullet popped out of her side as the wound healed. Soon enough Kai groaned and opened her eyes.

"Chosen?"

"Yeah." The injury finished healing and he stopped the flow of light magic. "You okay?"

She sat up slowly. "I am now, thank you."

"What happened?"

"Three soldiers were waiting in ambush, just as you feared. I followed them back to their base."

"Wait, they only sent three guys, no wizards or anything?" Conryu couldn't imagine that they thought three ordinary soldiers would be enough to capture or kill him.

"That's right, but these men had gray crystals that protected them from magic. I couldn't sense them even from a few feet away. It was like they didn't exist to my magical senses. I've never encountered anything like it. Anyway, I followed them to the military base but there was a barrier preventing me from entering through the borderland. I felt learning more about the crystal and the soldiers' mission worth the risk, so I snuck inside. Before I was spotted, I discovered that they plan to come after you again. Unfortunately, they didn't say where."

Conryu frowned and helped Kai to her feet. There was no way they could lure him into another trap, not with Jonny anyway. He paced through the knee-high grass as he considered the possibilities. No one would be stupid enough to go after his mother. If anyone laid a hand on her, he'd feed the entire government to Cerberus feet first, starting with the president.

Maria seemed like an unlikely target as well seeing as how she was at the Academy surrounded by wizards. He shook his head. He didn't have enough information to make a solid guess. Maybe Dean Blane and Maria had learned something about the crystal. He'd stop by the Academy and see. It would also be a good excuse to check on the security Kanna put in place.

CHAPTER 10

Merik paced in the dark listening to the distant sounds of battle. He hated not knowing what was going on, but by the time he reached a place where he could see the clearing, the battle would be over. A deep breath steadied his nerves. Merik had waited over a year to see Atlantis returned, he could wait a few more minutes.

Eventually, the explosions and gunfire stopped and a moment after that, the pressure in Merik's chest vanished. The ward was down; his pawns had succeeded.

*We are coming. Well done, Merik.*

When the voice confirmed his thoughts, Merik's heart soared. He'd done it. Soon he would get to meet the woman behind the voice. She had to be beautiful.

Forcing his way through the branches, Merik made his way toward the circle of stones. He had barely stepped into the clearing when he nearly tripped over a headless body. There were others, mostly intact, lying here and there. He ignored them and went straight for the stones.

Right in the center lay the bishop's body, his hand extended toward where Merik assumed the pillar would have appeared. The assassin's sword was jutting from the back of a nearby soldier. She'd certainly made a mess of his allies.

Activating the pillar must have been the bishop's final act before succumbing to his wounds. He had to give the man credit for determination if not brains.

A groan from behind him caused Merik to spin around. The assassin lay in a bloody heap on the dirt. She'd been shot more than once. Judging from the blood it was a miracle she was still alive. He walked over and retrieved her sword. It would be a fine thing to finish her off with her own weapon.

Merik kicked her over on her back, drawing another pained groan. She stared up at him as he placed her sword under her chin. He'd never killed anyone. He'd never even killed an animal, not with his own two hands. Running over a squirrel hardly counted. He found the idea of driving the blade home distasteful. She had already failed and her wounds would probably kill her in a few minutes anyway.

He tossed the sword aside. She wasn't worth his effort.

*Come Merik, we are all eager to meet you at last.*

He needed no further invitation. "Where are you?"

*Through the portal. Step into the center of the circle and your crystal will activate it.*

Leaving the dying assassin where she lay, he stepped over the bishop. The moment he did, a faint tingle ran through him, starting at his forehead where his crystals rested. There was a flash of light and a sense of movement.

The next thing he knew he was standing in a plaza surrounded by grass and trees. A circle of slowly dimming blue crystals surrounded him. In the distance crystal towers rose toward the sky. Beyond them a shimmering dome separated the city from whatever lay beyond.

So this was Atlantis. It was certainly alien. Beautiful, but like nothing he'd ever seen on earth.

"Welcome, Merik. I have been so looking forward to meeting you."

He knew that voice, only now it was in his ears and not his mind.

Merik turned slowly, wanting to savor the moment. He found himself face to face with a woman, and she was beautiful. She was also made of solid, clear crystal. Some sort of golden mist swirled and pulsed inside her crystal body like a nebula.

"Not what you were expecting?" Her crystal face was incapable of expression, but her tone suggested amusement.

"No, not exactly." Merik cleared his throat, trying to hide his disappointment. "Where are we?"

"In a space between realms. It will take time for Atlantis to fully return to the human realm. While we wait, I would show you the city and introduce you to your fellow Atlanteans."

Merik swallowed his anxiety and nodded. "I'd like that." He didn't want to end up a living statue, but hopefully that wouldn't be necessary.

She held out her hand and after a second of hesitation Merik took it. The crystal was warm, like a living person, but hard and smooth like glass. He'd never felt anything like it.

"I am Tanidel and it is nice to meet you, Merik."

She led him out of the park and toward the city proper. The streets were made of the same clear crystal as everything else. You could have heard a pin drop, so silent was Atlantis. Other than the steady tap of Tanidel's feet on the street, there wasn't another noise to be heard.

After five minutes of the unnerving quiet Merik asked, "Are there any people in these buildings?"

"Not anymore. Once thousands packed these towers, but thanks to the Lemurian cowards they are all gone."

"What happened?" Merik vaguely understood that there had been some sort of conflict between the two nations, but the details escaped him.

"We had our ways and they had theirs." Tanidel's shoulders rose and fell. "We lived on opposite sides of the world so there was no problem. Then one day an Atlantean explorer reached the edge of Lemurian territory. The so-called favored of the spirits feared our crystal magic. Since anyone could use it, they worried about what might happen if their vast underclass should gain access. They called us cursed by the spirits and went to war. Battles raged for decades, but we were winning. In desperation, the Lemurians summoned dark and evil magic. They hurled this curse at Atlantis. Thousands died and tens of thousands were sickened."

"That's horrible." Merik shuddered at the thought of such magic. The wizards he'd met were arrogant, but none struck him as evil. Desperate times and desperate measures he supposed.

"Our leaders forged the crystal shield and shifted Atlantis out of the human realm to this place. It exists outside of time. We hoped that would allow those sickened to survive until a cure could be found. Unfortunately, the disease was only slowed, not stopped and no cure was ever devised. Instead we were forced to build new bodies for ourselves and transfer our souls into them. We lost our humanity but gained immortality. We bought the time we needed to create unstoppable weapons which we could use to destroy the ancestors of Lemuria. Now that you have recalled us, the war can begin again. Only this time, we will win. Every Child of Lemuria will die."

Merik found his mouth had gone dry. They were going to

war against every wizard in the world. How could the survivors of Atlantis hope to win?

---

Jemma and two of her subordinate wizards flew through the night southeast toward Stonehenge. It seemed she'd barely returned from that ridiculous meeting with Conryu in Tokyo and gotten her research team working on the mysterious crystal when the nation's magical warning system had gone off. It signaled a massive arcane event, bigger even than the spell that Morgana used to destroy a big chunk of London. Hopefully they didn't find a smoking hole where Stonehenge used to be. The Ministry of Culture would have a fit.

They flew over a town, its lights winking in and out of sight, the people blissfully unaware that they might be facing yet another crisis. Some days she envied the average citizen whose biggest worry was losing their job or their kid getting sick. It would be great to only have to worry about a handful of people instead of an entire country.

Jemma turned to look at her second. "Any new information come in, Celia?"

Celia shook her head, sending her short blond hair every which way. "Not yet. The wizards on duty are still analyzing the pulse. It matched no known type of magic. Do you suppose Stonehenge has finally done whatever it was designed to do?"

Jemma swallowed a sigh. Theories abounded in regard to Stonehenge's true purpose. The Ministry had long known it was enchanted with some sort of protective spell, but since it never reacted to anything they did, the researchers assumed it was just left-over magic from some ancient ritual. It had become such a minor matter that they even allowed tourist visits. This should not have happened based on their current information

Why couldn't she have one problem to deal with at a time? That wasn't too much to ask, was it?

"I wish I knew," Jemma said at last.

The circle of stones was dark and silent when they arrived in the air above it. With her magically enhanced senses, Jemma easily made out the bodies littering the clearing. A faint flicker of life remained in one just inside the circle.

"Celia, check the stones. Emma, stabilize the survivor. I'll check the bodies."

A pair of "Yes, ma'ams" and her companions broke off. Jemma landed beside the first body and found it lacking a head. The cut was clean. An extremely sharp sword combined with plenty of muscle had taken this one out. She kicked the body over onto its back. He wore a vest that still held magazines for the rifle a few feet away as well as a pair of grenades. Whoever he was, he came ready for a fight.

She left the headless corpse and moved over to an intact one. The spell she planned to use required a body with a head.

Jemma raised her hands but before she could cast Celia said, "There's no magic left in the stones, Jemma. Whatever happened drained them dry."

Interesting. Usually a tiny spark would remain if the ancient spell was going to build up a new charge. If everything was gone then the magic was well and truly used up. That was usually a good thing. The stones were no longer a threat and she could stop worrying about them. The problem was, with nothing left to analyze, they might not know what the magic had done until it was too late.

She chanted in Infernal and a black mist rose out of the ground around the body before sliding down its throat. She wasn't calling its soul back, rather she was accessing the memories still stored in its brain. Whoever he was, he hadn't been dead long so she should get some coherent answers.

When the last of the mist had entered the body Jemma said, "Who are you?"

"Marko."

"Why did you come here?"

"To kill a wizard."

She frowned and glanced over at the stones where Emma was working healing magic on the survivor. Was that the wizard they'd come to kill? She wasn't one of Jemma's, so who was she?

Another mystery, that's who she was. Just what Jemma needed.

"Who do you serve?" she asked.

"The bishop."

Jemma's frown deepened. The bishop had to be a higher-up in the True Face of God. If those fanatics were involved, then things were worse than she'd feared. Why couldn't the bastards just leave the Kingdom alone? Maybe this was payback for her sending Conryu to rescue those girls. Maybe, but that didn't feel right.

She altered the spell, binding the magic in place and using it to preserve the body. If more questions came up, she didn't want his brain to deteriorate before she could ask them.

"I found the leader." Celia dragged a body out of the circle and dropped it at Jemma's feet.

He had a gold cross necklace signifying his position in the cult. She couldn't remember the exact rank, but gold had to be pretty high up. No doubt MI6 could give her all the information she'd need.

Jemma cast her spell a second time to preserve the bishop in case she needed to question him later.

"How far out is the clean-up team?" Jemma asked.

Celia checked her watch. "About fifteen minutes. The Ministry of Defense is going to have a field day with this. We've been invaded twice in as many years. Not a good look for them. It's not like we didn't offer to set up a ring of wards around the entire island to watch for incoming ships."

Jemma grunted. Ministerial rivalries didn't interest her. As far as she was concerned, they were all working toward the same goal, keeping the Kingdom safe. Unfortunately, she knew many of her fellow ministers felt differently. Hopefully they wouldn't make pointless demands and argue over jurisdiction.

"How's the survivor?" Jemma asked.

"Very lucky," Emma said. "Given the number of bullets and pieces of shrapnel that hit her, it's a miracle none pierced anything vital. She's stable, but I'm going to need a couple days to fully heal her."

A couple days. Jemma hoped they had that long.

## CHAPTER 11

The safest way for Conryu to enter the Academy was by using his library. And that was exactly what he was going to do, but first he opened a Hell portal and traveled to the edge of the campus. He found the first ninja on duty a few seconds later. The only part of her that stood out against the infinite darkness were her eyes which seemed to glitter with an inner light. She bowed as he approached.

"All quiet, Chosen," she said.

A weight lifted off his chest. While Conryu hadn't really expected trouble, it was good to have confirmation. "How many of you did Kanna assign to this mission?"

"Ten. She thought that would be enough to watch the perimeter and if necessary, deal with any threats. We're working on one-week shifts so no one will get too bored."

"Good, thank you."

She bowed again and Conryu summoned the library door. He and Kai entered and with a thought he moved them to Maria's room. A quick peek revealed her roommate sound asleep and Maria's bed empty. He grinned, not surprised in the least. Another mental command shifted them to the library.

Sure enough there she was, three open books on the table in front of her along with the clear crystal. She wore her white student's robe and had her feet tucked up under her.

Not wanting to scare her to death, Conryu rapped on the library door before he and Kai emerged. She looked up and frowned, not the reaction he'd hoped for.

"This thing is impossible," she said without preamble. "I've read everything I can think of, cast every spell, and nothing. Even Dean Blane can't get a read on it. How did those ignorant clods get their hands on something so rare?"

"If I knew that, I'd just ask whoever gave it to them," Conryu said. "Everything okay here otherwise?"

She fully focused on him. "Why do you ask?"

He told her about Jonny and the soldiers threatening to take another run at him. "I didn't know if they might try something with you. I've got a group of Kai's fellow ninjas keeping an eye on everyone, but if these guys have crystals that make them immune to magic, they might not sense them before it's too late."

"More crystals," Maria said. "It can't be a coincidence. And Jonny, I can't believe he'd betray you like that."

"I couldn't either, but it wasn't his idea. Still, I took his rune stone so the generals can't use him again. Anyway, I don't think the crystals are a coincidence either. My original plan was to keep Jemma in the dark about your research, but now I wonder if we shouldn't pool our resources."

Maria snorted. "If we can't figure out what these things are, I doubt the Ministry is having any better luck. Still, I suppose it couldn't hurt to reach out. I'll mention your suggestion to Dean Blane in the morning. What will you do now?"

"I was thinking I'd head back to the island to get a little…"

He trailed off as he thought of something. Conryu smacked his forehead. "The island. They have to know I'm basically living there. It's the one place I'll return to eventually that they can attack without drawing attention."

"But the barrier," Maria said.

"If their crystals make them immune to magic, they can probably pass right through it. That's got to be their plan." Conryu kissed Maria on the cheek. "I've got to go. See you later."

"Be careful."

He waved over his shoulder as they returned to the library. Before the enemy showed up, he'd need reinforcements.

It never ceased to amaze Conryu just how much you could accomplish with magic. He, Kai, and six extra ninjas had returned to the floating island four hours ago. Now, in the clearing that held his workshop, was a simple three-room log cabin complete with rustic furniture, all made with magic and nearby trees. Prime had been thoroughly disgusted that he'd used his power for something so mundane, but if he wanted to set a trap, he needed a target. Since he usually slept in the library, Conryu had never bothered building a house.

"What now, Chosen?" Kai asked.

"Now we wait. I suspect they won't make a move until night. And it may not even be this night. We have no way of knowing. Given my complete lack of other leads, we'll just have to be patient. Is everyone in place?"

"Yes, if the enemy appears, they will not escape us."

"Great." Conryu summoned the library door and they entered. Once inside he created a recliner for each of them then added a viewing window that looked down on the cabin. They'd be able to see everything in comfort and safety.

"Will they be visible given their immunity to magic?" Kai asked.

"Beats me, but the cabin door opening will let us know if they are invisible."

She nodded and settled gingerly into the chair. Anything resembling comfort seemed to make her uneasy, like a cushion would make her weak. It was a strange thing, but he'd at least convinced her that it was okay to sit down when he was around. Before she always insisted on standing in his presence.

"You take first watch." He closed his eyes. "I'm going to take a nap."

Sometime later, Kai shook him awake. Conryu groaned and rubbed his eyes.

"Someone is here, Chosen," Kai said.

He studied the image. Night had fallen, but the library's magic allowed him to see as if it was daylight. Despite that, he saw nothing. "You sure?"

"Watch the grass." She pointed and he immediately noticed footsteps appearing.

Once he knew what to look for, it was simple to spot the remaining two paths approaching his cabin. Their backup had strict instructions not to strike until he gave the signal.

The front door opened. Conryu counted slowly to three then snapped his fingers. The fire magic he'd woven into the cabin exploded, sending chunks of burning wood flying everywhere. Seconds later Conryu and Kai rushed out of the library.

They found the two men that remained outside lying on the ground with black swords at their throats. Magic or not, that razor-sharp steel would kill with no trouble.

"Where's the third guy?" Conryu asked.

One of the ninjas pointed toward the flaming wreckage. He

gestured and the fires vanished. A body lay unmoving in the center of the debris. Conryu took a step towards it and Kai said, "Careful, Chosen, he might be faking."

Since the unlucky soldier's face was pierced with shards of timber a foot long, Conryu seriously doubted he was pretending. In fact, he hadn't seen many bodies that looked deader than this poor bastard.

Conryu grabbed a stray piece of wood and shaped it into a pair of tongs. Touching an anti-magic crystal didn't seem prudent for a wizard. He poked around and finally got the charred uniform moved aside enough to retrieve the gray amulet. It was about three inches long and ended in a point, like someone had hacked it free from a larger piece. Absurd of course. You couldn't hack stone.

A simple earth magic spell that should have revealed the sort of stone it was, vanished the instant the energy made contact with the crystal.

Remarkable. At least when he cast that spell on the clear crystal it had given a response. Not that unknown material was much more valuable than nothing.

He carried the crystal outside the wreckage and set it in the grass before stepping back. A line of fire lanced out from his finger and burned a path toward the crystal. A foot out it vanished as completely as the earth magic spell. That gave him a rough idea of the item's range. Basically far enough to protect a single person. Useful, but hardly an overwhelming advantage.

"Chosen, what should we do with the prisoners?" Kai asked.

He'd been so wrapped up in his experiment, Conryu had momentarily forgotten them. "Get their crystals, careful not to touch them, and add them to the pile over here. Once that's done, I'll question them."

"We won't tell you anything," one of the soldiers said.

Conryu smiled. Clearly, he'd never been questioned by a wizard. Another burst of earth magic wrapped the survivors in vines at the same time they were forced to their feet. When he was finished, only their heads were visible through the greenery.

He walked over and raised a glowing hand. "Now, let's have a look at what you're hiding in there."

When his hand touched the first man's forehead, light magic surged into his brain, taking Conryu's consciousness along for the ride. He followed the soldier's memories from the moment of the explosion backward. They'd arrived by plane and with the crystal's power, passed easily through the floating island's barrier.

Conryu had sensed no change in the energy flow, so the crystals had done no lasting damage. That was good. He didn't want an endless stream of unwelcome company falling out of the sky into his lap.

The memories retreated further. There was a briefing where they were given orders to kill him. The soldier had been confident that they could complete the mission no problem. Taking out some inexperienced kid should be simple. Clearly this guy hadn't paid attention when he was given background on his target, assuming they'd gotten a background briefing. When it came to combat, Conryu had seen more than his share.

Conryu didn't recognize the older man in uniform that gave the order, but then he hadn't had much contact with the military. His name, according to the memory Conryu was reading, was General Smith. He ran the entire special operations department of the military. The memory of the old man held warmth and respect. The soldier held his commanding officer in high regard.

A quick skim made it clear that the soldier had no idea

where the crystals came from beyond the Research and Development division, which was held in considerably lower regard than the general. That was no help at all. Conryu suspected General Smith would have more useful information.

He released the spell and after a moment of disorientation stepped away from the prisoner. He'd never used that particular spell before and wasn't anxious to do so again. He couldn't deny its usefulness but rummaging around in someone's brain felt like the ultimate invasion of privacy.

"Shall we kill them, Chosen?" one of the new ninjas asked.

"Certainly not. We're going to visit their boss. And it's only polite to bring a gift when you go visiting."

## CHAPTER 12

Malice Kincade hobbled down the hall of the presidential residence toward the president's private office. The white walls decorated with generic art didn't interest her. Her cane tapped along on the gray marble floor, each impact making her grimace harder and hate it more. She had only started using the damn thing a few days after the madness of Morgana's attack. Her hip kept slipping in and out and she nearly fell twice.

Magical healing could do nothing for her. The light magic users said it was old age and there was no cure for it. Blithering idiots. There were always cures, just not in their discipline. She had some less moralistic wizards looking at several. For now, she was reduced to limping around like an invalid. At least her cane held enough magic to make anyone that thought her a weak target regret their stupidity, for the few seconds that remained of their life.

Speaking of people that believed her weak, the president had called today's meeting without informing her. Their relationship hadn't been great before the attack and it was worse now. He wanted to replace her but didn't dare. The government and Kincade Magical Industries were too deeply entwined. He needed her and he knew it. But he didn't like it.

Worse, as far as she was concerned, the Department of Research and Development was involved with a secret, magic-involved project and she knew next to nothing about it. Her people in the department were trying to ferret out what was going on, but so far, they'd come up empty.

She suspected that whoever was in charge of security over there now had figured out whose true loyalty was to Malice and marginalized them. It spoke to their skill that she didn't even know who that person was.

But that was a problem for another time. She rounded a corner and limped toward the two soldiers on duty outside the office. They immediately snapped to attention.

When she got closer, they shifted to block her. "The president is in a private meeting. He gave instructions not to be disturbed."

Malice looked from one to the other, but neither could meet her cold glare. Children, the both of them. Standing guard with their worthless rifles. Neither of them would have a hope in hell of stopping even a weak wizard, much less Malice.

Unfortunately, satisfying as killing them both would be, it wouldn't advance her cause today. "I'll wait," she said.

A hard bench sat across the hall from the office door. She sat and closed her eyes. The office was warded against eavesdropping, but what Malice doubted anyone but her realized was that the one hired to perform the enchantment worked for a Kincade subsidiary. She knew exactly how the wards worked and exactly how to bypass them.

Malice shifted her hands to her lap and subtly rubbed the gold ring on her right hand. The magic woven into the metal came to life, sending her awareness up and out of her body. The wards appeared as a maze of lines filling the air around the room. She concentrated and performed a precise gesture with her ethereal hands, a gesture that would have been difficult with her real hands given the arthritis twisting her knuckles.

The lines bent out of her way and she flew through the gap. Inside she found the president, his hair more gray than brown now, seated at the head of a long table along with several cabinet members and other high-ranking advisors. Malice knew all of them and she knew they must all be wondering where she was.

Another individual, this one a stranger to her, stood at the front of the room. He was dressed in a lab coat as though he'd come directly from his work. In truth she knew the scientists liked to wear those coats because they thought it convinced the higher-ups that they knew what they were talking about.

It didn't, but no one ever corrected them.

On the white board beside him was a picture of a gray crystal shaped roughly like an obelisk. She'd never seen one and had no idea what it was or why it would be of any interest to the powerful men gathered here.

"Have you made any progress in duplicating the crystal?" the president asked.

The scientist looked everywhere but at his boss. "No, sir. We haven't isolated how it works so we can't duplicate the effect."

The president slammed his fist on the table. His frustration brought a smile to Malice's ethereal face. "Gaining the ability to negate magic is the key to ending our dependence on wizards. After the attack, your budget was increased to basically unlimited and in two months you've made no progress.

What the hell have you been spending those millions on, doughnuts?"

"I'm sorry, sir. But without understanding the mechanism by which the crystal functions, we can't even begin to guess how to copy it."

Malice had heard enough. Any amusement she might have felt at the president's frustration was overshadowed by what he was attempting. Creating an artifact capable of negating magic was tantamount to declaring war on all the wizards in the world. No wonder he didn't want Malice to know what he was working on. She would have done everything in her power to put a stop to it.

The weight and pain of her worn-out body settled around her spirit and she stood.

The guards shot her a nervous side-eye as she struggled to her feet. Malice ignored them and shuffled back the way she'd come. She might not have had her meeting, but she learned more than enough.

If the president wanted to declare himself the enemy of all wizards, Malice wouldn't take the threat lying down.

As Tanidel led him through the silent crystal city, Merik couldn't help wondering what Atlantis was like at the height of its power. He pictured tall, graceful people in white robes with crystals in their foreheads walking here and there, discussing matters of importance. There had to be workers as well. No culture could survive without industry, but he had trouble squaring that necessity with the wonder all around him.

His guide finally turned off the street and angled toward a rosy pink tower. The building appeared to be solid crystal, but as they approached a door formed to allow them inside. The interior was every bit as remarkable as the outside. The chairs and tables appeared grown out of the floor. There was a desk to one side where a secretary would have sat had this been an office building. Instead the space was empty, just like everything else.

"This way." Tanidel walked over to a blank section of wall.

As she approached, the wall opened just like the outside wall. It was a neat trick, but how would a visitor know where to go? Then again maybe that was intentional. At this point, a visitor wasn't likely to be friendly so keeping them lost would be an advantage.

Merik followed her into a large boardroom with a round table around which sat eleven people, all made of crystal like Tanidel. Everyone stood to greet them.

"Merik," Tanidel said. "Allow me to introduce the survivors of Atlantis."

He was struck momentarily dumb. Twelve people? There were only twelve survivors of Atlantis? How in the world could they hope to go to war with all the wizards in the world?

"It is a pleasure to meet you, brother," one of the male Atlanteans said.

Merik shook his cold, hard hand. The men, he wasn't even sure if they were men at this point, but close enough. They were built like Greek statues, with perfect crystal features. The same features, Merik realized. The seven men all looked exactly the same, as did the five women.

"We are beyond grateful for what you've done," one of the women said.

"I'm glad I could help," Merik said. "All my life I've felt like I didn't really fit in. Now I know why. Are there others like me?"

"Very few," one of the men said. "When we've dealt with the wizards, we will find them and bring them into the fold."

"About that. Twelve against thousands doesn't seem like a fair fight. How can you hope to defeat so many given your limited numbers?"

"Our numbers may be limited," a woman said. He was really going to have to learn their names, not that he could tell them apart. "But as you've seen, there are many in the world that hate, fear, or resent the wizards. If we offer them a way to defeat their enemy, finding people willing to fight will be easy. Please, sit with us."

At her invitation, two chairs grew out of the floor. Merik took one and Tanidel the other. Their chairs were every bit as hard as their flesh. Merik shuddered to think what he'd find when he went to sleep tonight.

"Do you all have names?" Merik asked.

"Of course," one of the men said. "But we haven't bothered with them since transitioning to our new forms. We recognize each other by our unique vibrations now. I'm sure for someone still of flesh and blood, this is a difficult concept to grasp. That is why we designated the one you know as Tanidel as our representative to our brothers and sisters in the human realm. She is perhaps the only one of us that still has a grasp of her old self."

"So how should I address you?" Merik asked.

"It would be easiest if you simply asked your questions to the group and whoever has the answer will reply. Should you wish to speak with one of us in particular, focus on them and we will sense your desire through the crystal in your forehead."

This was going to take some getting used to. "What happens now?"

"We wait. Until Atlantis has fully returned to the human realm, we can do nothing."

"And when it does?" Merik asked.

"We will make contact with the potential allies you have

found for us. They in turn will no doubt suggest others of like mind. We will build an army and hunt our enemies to extinction, just as they would have done to us."

And that was the crux of the matter. "How? There are a lot of wizards out there."

Another Atlantean said, "You know the crystal that renders you immune to magic? That was only a prototype, a crude artifact created at the end of the war. In the thousands of years since we have perfected the weapon. Now we can create entire zones where magic will not function. Each of us is now a magic-negating crystal able to project that effect over one hundred yards. We can protect a sizable force who will in turn cut down our foes."

"But you must be tired. Tanidel will take you to a place where you can rest. We will speak again soon."

They all stood.

Merik had been to enough corporate meetings to know when he was being dismissed. Despite their claims of brotherhood, they clearly considered themselves superior to Merik. Perhaps because they were pure crystal and he was still flesh and blood.

Either way, he followed Tanidel out of the boardroom feeling a good deal less confident than he had when he arrived.

## CHAPTER 13

According to the information Conryu extracted from the commandos, General Smith was waiting for his assassins to report in at Jonny's base in Florida. It was still dark when Conryu, Kai, her fellow ninjas, and their two prisoners appeared a quarter mile up the street from the base.

Conryu cast a basic detection spell. Just as Kai warned him, the base was heavily warded against any kind of magical trespass. Someone had spent weeks if not months layering wards around the huge complex.

Boy was whoever did that going to be pissed when he got done.

Conryu took up his staff and the crystal instantly turned black as it sensed his desire. He channeled a huge quantity of dark magic into it before releasing the energy in a massive Dispel Magic blast. Like a wave hitting a sandcastle, his spell washed away every trace of magical protection around the base.

He glanced at Kai. "Okay."

She and her fellow ninjas vanished into the borderland. They would keep a lookout there and deal with anyone that might be a threat to him. Not that he expected that to be an issue.

Shifting from dark magic to earth magic, he wove several defensive spells, mingling them with light magic enhancements. By the time he finished, a tank blast wouldn't scratch him. With his precautious taken, Conryu pointed at his bound prisoners. They floated off the ground and followed along at his heel like an obedient hound as he walked straight up to the main gate.

A pair of guards raised their rifles as he approached. "Halt!" one of the men said. It would have been more impressive if his voice hadn't quavered.

Conryu obliged. "I'm here to see General Smith. He sent some trash to my house. I came to return it."

"N…Name?"

"Conryu Koda. The general will want to see me. You shouldn't keep him waiting."

The guards looked at each other and one finally ran to their shack to make a call. The second kept his rifle pointed at Conryu. Not that he was worried about a simple bullet, but just to be safe, Conryu used a tiny spark of dark magic to disintegrate the weapon's firing pin.

Minutes later a veritable military parade came rushing toward the gate. There were jeeps with machine guns mounted on them, soldiers with rocket launchers and flame throwers, and about two hundred infantry men armed with rifles identical to the one currently pointed at his chest. He spotted Jonny in the group of infantry but put him out of his mind. His friend had made his choice. Now he'd have to accept the consequences.

If you ignored the fact that a thought from him would leave

them all unarmed or dead, the display was impressive. When they had taken up position facing him, their useless weapons all focused his way, an officer in a tan uniform jumped out of a jeep and marched up to face him.

"You're under arrest," the officer said.

Conryu restrained a laugh. "On what charge?"

"Trespassing on military property."

Conryu looked left and right. "I'm still outside the base. Look, I came here to talk to a general, not to a whatever you are. Why don't you go get your boss so we can discuss our differences rationally?"

"My orders are to take you into custody."

Conryu swallowed a sigh. "Go to sleep."

A pulse of light magic rushed out. The moment it hit the gathered soldiers they collapsed, out cold. In less than a second, only Conryu and the officer were still standing. "Do you want to take me to him now or do you want to take a nap with your men while I search on my own?"

All the blood had drained from the officer's face. "General Smith isn't going to be pleased if I bring you to him."

"Good. I'm not especially pleased that he sent three men to kill me. Now, I'm going to give you three seconds to start walking before I knock you out and do it myself. One."

"Okay, okay. It'll probably mean my career but come along."

The officer set out and Conryu fell in behind him. They walked around the unconscious soldiers and headed deeper into the base. There were buildings and training areas everywhere. But no more soldiers presented themselves. That was good. He didn't worry about Kai doing anything unfortunate, but the new girls were still killers at heart. If they thought he was in danger, they were likely to cut first and ask questions later.

They finally reached a modest building near the center of

the base. It wasn't much bigger than the apartment where Conryu grew up. He sensed a single person inside, so no ambush. His guide rapped on the door and a moment later General Smith, looking exactly as he did in the memories Conryu saw, opened the door.

"Major Evans," the general said. "My order was clear was it not?"

"Perfectly, sir. Unfortunately, I lack the means to carry them out. Our…visitor wishes to speak with you."

"And if I don't wish to speak with him?"

Conryu had had about enough of this.

"Then you can shut up and listen." He pointed and the bound soldiers landed in a heap in front of the general's door. "Your stupidity already got one man killed. Had I been so inclined I could have dealt with these two the same way. Lucky for you, I'm not violent by nature."

"These men were wearing items of great value to the Alliance. Where are they?"

"Safe, where no one will ever see them again. Where, exactly, did you get them?"

"That's classified."

"Figured you'd say something unhelpful like that." Conryu paralyzed both men with a thought and moved closer to the general.

Distasteful as it was, the only way he was going to get the answers he needed was to take them. He touched the general's forehead and activated the spell he'd used earlier on his assassin. There were a bunch of meetings, some scientists, a visit with the president.

Here we go. Another scientist, this one older than the rest. No name appeared in the memory. The scientist handed the general a metal box with the three crystals inside. Whoever that scientist was, Conryu needed to find him.

When he had ended his spell Conryu said, "Leave me alone, General, and I will return the favor. Come after me again and next time I'll send you bodies."

With that final warning, Conryu vanished into the borderland.

Murmured voices slowly dragged Sienna back to awareness. As she came awake the scent of antiseptic stung her nose. She was in a hospital, she knew that before she opened her eyes. By some miracle she'd survived getting shot multiple times. The pain of her wounds was gone. Only magic could have healed her so completely. That meant she wasn't a prisoner of the Atlanteans. The arrogant man must have deemed her no longer a threat.

He would come to regret that decision. Sienna may have failed in her mission to stop the return of Atlantis, but she could still help make things right. If it cost her life, she would make the bastard regret sparing her.

"Good morning," a cheery voice said.

Sienna slowly opened her eyes and found a middle-aged woman in a white robe standing over her, a clipboard in her hand. "Where am I?"

"The Ministry of Magic's infirmary. When we found you, someone had put a bunch of holes in you. Had we arrived a moment later, you likely would have died. Can you tell us what happened?"

"Can I get something to drink?" Sienna asked to buy herself some time.

"Of course. I'll be right back." The light magic wizard – she could be nothing else – walked away.

Sienna tilted her head a fraction to get a better idea where she was. It looked like a typical hospital room, maybe thirty feet square, a bathroom near the door, a little stand near her bed, all very clean and ordinary. The only thing missing was a tv.

She threw her blankets aside and sat up. A chill breeze ran up her spine. All she had on was a gown that felt like it was made of tissue paper. Her shoes were missing as well. Everything seemed to be working okay at least. Escaping this place in her current state wouldn't be easy.

And maybe she shouldn't try. Sienna might not know a lot about world affairs, but she knew enough to know when Atlantis returned, these would be some of the people on the front line fighting them. They could use all the help they could get and even then, it might not be enough. Her ancestors barely drove the enemy away long ago. She wasn't sure if modern wizards were up to the task.

The wizard returned as she was making up her mind, a paper cup in one hand and a foam pitcher in the other. "Here we are, water. Lunch will be served in an hour or so. It's not the best, but I expect you're hungry. Patients are always hungry after magical healing."

Sienna took a sip of the water and made up her mind. "I wish to speak with whoever's in charge here. A great threat is approaching this world. You must be ready to face it."

Jemma drummed her fingers on her desk as she listened to Dean Blane run through the list of tests she'd run on the inscrutable crystal Conryu had acquired for her. The list very closely resembled the one Jemma's team had performed with equally worthless results. If someone as brilliant as Dean Blane hadn't gotten anywhere in analyzing the crystal, her team's lack of results didn't seem so bad.

What annoyed her was that no one else was supposed to have a crystal in the first place. Conryu was supposed to bring them to her. Of course, her information said nothing about there being multiple stones in the fanatics' possession, so she hadn't even known about them before answering the phone.

When she finally finished Dean Blane said, "I think we should pool our resources. Whatever we're dealing with is outside my understanding of magic."

Given the research department's complete failure to date, Jemma was in no position to turn down an offer of assistance. "Agreed. But whatever we do will have to be just between us, our governments are still not on the best of terms."

"I prefer to keep them out of it anyway. In my experience the government tends to do more harm than good in these sorts of situations. I'll be in touch."

Jemma hung up the phone and sighed. It felt like things were getting out of hand. She hated it when she did not have complete control, not that she ever seemed to. As she was pondering her next move, her office door opened.

Celia poked her head in and said, "The mystery wizard is finally awake and she's asking to talk to you."

"What does she want to talk about?"

"You're going to love this; she says there's a great threat coming and that we need to be ready to deal with it."

Jemma rubbed the bridge of her nose. How come nobody ever wanted to talk to her about a nice quiet dinner and a bottle of wine?

"Does she seem sane, or is this going to be a waste of my time?"

Celia shrugged. "She's not bouncing off the walls crazy, but whether she has anything useful to tell us I couldn't say. Will you see her?"

Jemma pushed away from her desk and stood. "I might as well."

The infirmary was three floors down from her office. She and Celia made the walk in silence. Jemma couldn't deny her curiosity about where the woman came from. While she was unconscious, the Ministry had done a number of tests and searches and as far as they could figure out, she'd appeared out of thin air. The sword they found nearby was a mystery as well. As best they could figure, it dated to six thousand years ago.

The head healer guided them past a trio of empty rooms and in to see the infirmary's sole patient. She was sitting on the edge of her bed, a cheap department robe wrapped around her shoulders. Considering the shape she'd been in the last time Jemma saw her, she looked remarkably healthy.

The wizard looked from Jemma to Celia. "Which of you is master of this place?"

"I lead the Ministry of Magic," Jemma said. "I'm told you wanted to speak with me. Perhaps you could start with your name and why you were at Stonehenge with a group of terrorists?"

"My name is Sienna and I was there to stop them. I nearly succeeded. But nearly succeeding is the same as total failure. Soon the enemy of all wizards will return. Atlantis is coming and you must prepare yourselves."

Jemma wanted to grimace but kept her expression neutral. Looked like this was going to be a waste of time after all.

"You don't believe me," Sienna said.

"Atlantis is a myth," Celia said.

Sienna smiled. "So was a male wizard until three years ago. If I'd come to you twenty years ago and said soon the most powerful wizard in the world will be born and it will be a boy, you would have laughed me out of here or locked me in a padded cell, but it happened all the same. Atlantis is coming and they will resume the ancient war with the heirs of Lemuria."

This strange wizard had a point. Everything she said about Conryu was true. No one believed it was possible until it happened. Jemma couldn't afford to be so closed-minded that she ignored a potential threat. The Atlantis from the stories might be a myth, but that didn't mean there wasn't an Atlantis that the stories were based on.

"Tell me everything," Jemma said.

"Everything is going to take a while. It started with a war thousands of years ago. Lemuria, the first kingdom of magic, home to the ancestors of what would become modern wizards, fought a drawn-out battle with Atlantis, a city that used a different form of magic, one based on crystals and usable by everyone, not just those chosen by the spirits."

At the mention of crystals, Jemma's focus sharpened. "How do these crystals work?"

Sienna shook her head. "If my ancestors ever knew, the knowledge was lost or buried long ago. I only know that the two forms were incompatible and the practitioners of one sort of magic generally didn't get along with the other."

"Didn't get along?" Celia asked.

"Yes. When a Lemurian encountered someone from Atlantis, only one of them tended to walk away alive."

"What about Stonehenge?" Jemma asked.

"When Atlantis vanished from the human realm," Sienna said, "they left a tether so they could use it to return after rebuilding their strength. The Lemurians, despite their considerable power, couldn't destroy it. They were forced to erect a barrier that would stop anyone with Atlantean blood from approaching. The standing stones served as a focus for the spell."

Jemma spoke with Sienna for several hours before finally excusing herself. When they were alone Celia asked, "Do you believe her?"

"If she's lying, it is the most elaborate charade I've ever encountered. And to what purpose? She's asked us for nothing. Sienna nearly died trying to stop the cultists from entering Stonehenge. That's a long way to go for a deception." Jemma shook her head. "I think she's telling the truth, at least the truth as she understands it."

"What are we going to do?" Celia asked.

"That is indeed the question." Even with everything they'd learned from Sienna, Jemma still had no real idea how the "crystal magic" as she called it worked.

How did you defeat an enemy armed with a weapon you didn't understand?

CHAPTER 14

After putting General Smith and his assassins to sleep, Conryu and Kai stepped into the library and he shifted them to Sentinel City. His mother worked in the weapons research department and he hoped she might recognize the older man that provided the crystals. If she didn't, he wasn't sure what their next move would be.

Conryu didn't bother creating chairs for them since the transfer would only take seconds. As they stood in front of the door Kai asked, "Was it wise to leave the general and his men alive, Chosen?"

"Of course it wasn't wise," Prime answered. "My master is as soft as a century-old corpse. I've argued many times that he would be better off killing all his enemies, but he insists that killing is only a last resort. He doesn't really even mean it when he threatens people."

"Don't hold back, Prime," Conryu said. "Tell us how you really feel. Look, even if I murdered the general and his men, what difference would it make? Do you think he's the only general they've got? Or that those are the only soldiers? All I'd accomplish is making the government madder at me than they already are. Besides, the crystals were the real threat. Without their magic-negating abilities, even the best soldiers are barely a nuisance to me."

Conryu rapped twice on the doors to let his mother know they were there and opened them. It was quite late, but knowing her, she was still up working on some project or other. Since his father died, she'd been even more obsessed with work. Conryu figured it was to take her mind off being lonely. He'd offered to bring her to the island, but she always passed. And it wasn't like he could stay at home, not with the government breathing down his neck.

It sucked, but he didn't have a ton of good options.

He and Kai stepped into the apartment. It was dark and for a moment he feared maybe she really was asleep, then he spotted the light from under the door to his old bedroom. She had converted it into a home office.

"Mom?"

The door opened and his mother stood in the doorway wearing a blue bathrobe, her matching slippers sticking out from underneath. Her cheeks were hollow and she had dark circles under her eyes. Looked like she'd been skipping meals and not sleeping again. Maria's mother tried to keep an eye on her, but there was only so much Shizuku could do.

"Hello, dear. It's late, shouldn't you be asleep?"

Conryu smiled. "Pot calling the kettle black?"

She shrugged and he crossed the living room to hug her. She felt thin in his arms. Once this crystal business was dealt with, they were going to have to make some serious changes. She couldn't go on like this and he couldn't let her.

When he stepped back, she said, "You're not here to socialize at this time of night. What brings you by?"

"I'm hoping you can help me." Conryu conjured an image of

the man he'd seen in the general's memory. "Do you know this guy?"

"Of course I know him," his mother said. "He's my boss. His name is Connel Ames and he's a brilliant researcher. We're working on a new project, a form of magical technology based on crystals. We're trying to isolate exactly how the item we acquired functions, with limited success I must admit. Connel thinks it works based on some form of energy manipulation, like standard spells, but I'm convinced vibrations are the key. The crystal vibrates at a constant pitch, never varying or stopping. I've never encountered anything like it. How do you know him?"

Conryu took a deep breath to steady himself. Learning his mother was working on the crystals was a surprise to say the least. "He gave three gray crystals to a general named Smith who in turn gave them to three special ops guys who tried to kill me, twice. The crystals negate magic."

His mother stared at him, her tired eyes wide. "Oh my god. I didn't know. I would have warned you. It's just I thought if we had a way of stopping magic then your father…"

Conryu hugged her again. "It's okay, Mom."

She cried against his chest, but not for long. She was always the practical one. "I'm okay now."

He let her go and asked, "Do you know where he got the crystals in the first place?"

"They came in the mail."

"In the mail? Are you kidding?"

"No, at least that's what I was told. Why would Connel lie?"

Conryu could think of several reasons, including protecting his source. "We need to talk to him. Are there any more crystals?"

"Just the one we've been working on. It's locked up tight in the vault in the basement. I don't have a key."

"Do you know where Connel lives? I have a few questions."

She shook her head. "I don't. We never talk about personal things, only work. He comes in at five in the morning. You could catch him in the car park. There are cameras, but that shouldn't be a problem for you."

"I think you should call in sick tomorrow, Mom."

"I'm going to quit. Using my research to try and kill my son? No, I won't accept that. Maybe I'll take you up on that offer to visit your island."

"What time is it?" Conryu asked.

"Just after midnight." For some reason Prime always knew exactly what time it was. Probably something to do with being a demon.

"In five hours, we finally get some answers." Conryu could hardly wait.

---

Connel Ames was shorter than Conryu expected. As the researcher got out of his midlife-crisis convertible, Conryu figured he wasn't much more than five ten. A scruff of gray beard covered his cheeks and he had the same dark ridges under his eyes that Conryu's mother did. Neither of them seemed to be getting enough sleep.

A single camera covered the area of the parking lot where Connel put his car. Conryu waited in the library until Kai deactivated it. Sure enough five seconds later Kai appeared and gave him a thumbs up. That was his cue.

Conryu opened the door and stepped into the real world directly in front of Connel. The scientist flinched and took a step back. He looked like he wanted to run, but Kai appeared behind him, a hand on her sword, making it clear that escape was not an option.

"What do you want?" Connel asked.

"You know me?" Conryu asked.

"Everyone knows you. Your mother also keeps a picture of you on her desk. Very unprofessional. What do you want? I have a lot of work to do."

"Your work is what brings me here today." Conryu moved a step closer. "Where did you get the crystals?"

"She shouldn't have told you about those. Our research is top secret. If you'll excuse me." Connel tried to walk away, but at Conryu's command, the stone gripped his feet, locking him in place.

"Mom didn't tell me about your research. Three soldiers with magic-negating crystals tried to kill me. I saw you give them to General Smith. Where did they come from?"

"I received a package in the mail. Four matching crystals were inside. On my desk at home I keep a magical toy, very old, been in the family for years. As soon as the crystals got close it deactivated. The moment I saw what they did, I realized this was a discovery that would make my career. Truly I have no idea who my benefactor was. Should the opportunity arise, I would be delighted to thank him or her."

Conryu sensed no lies in his story. Still, he couldn't imagine why anyone would give away something as valuable as the crystals. Clearly the answer wasn't going to come from Connel.

"My mother won't be coming in today or ever again. Consider this her resignation."

"No!" He lunged, coming out of his shoes to grab Conryu's arm as he stepped away.

Kai's sword was at his throat in an instant.

Conryu waved her back. "Why not? You're the head researcher, what's so important about my mother?"

"We're pursuing parallel tracks. I don't know which of us

will turn out to be correct, but if I have to do her work as well as mine, it will set the project back months."

Conryu raised an eyebrow.

Connel looked away. "I don't have months. My superiors are growing impatient. They want a functioning replica of the crystal soon, or they're taking the project from my department and moving it to the lab in Central. You know what that means? My career will be ruined. You don't walk away from a failure of this scale with no consequences. I may never get another opportunity this huge. Please, convince her to change her mind."

"Not much chance of that after the military used your toys to try and kill me. How long before they try again, this time with a hundred magic-proof guys? I don't think so."

He slumped. "Then I'm doomed."

"Mom says you're pretty bright. I'm sure you'll figure something out. Let's go, Kai."

They entered the library and Conryu immediately conjured a viewing window. Connel recovered quickly, retrieving his shoes and hurrying toward the Science Department building. Conryu willed the library to follow him and as he hoped, the building's wards couldn't stop the library's unique magic from entering. It seemed the government used the same sort of magic that Shizuku used to protect the apartment building. Pretty standard and generally effective, but not against everything.

They followed him through empty halls to an equally empty lab filled with tables, computers, and all manner of technical things Conryu couldn't begin to name. Connel went straight to a massive metal door and punched a ten-digit code into the control panel. Next he stared into an opening while a scanner ran over his open eye.

The door swung ponderously open and Connel went in. He

was back out seconds later with a rectangular case. When he reached his desk, he removed a gray crystal that was a twin to the ones the assassins carried.

"Ready, Kai?"

She nodded. Conryu backed into a dark corner and opened the library door. Kai slipped out, silent as a shadow. Not that Connel would have noticed if she started playing the trumpet right in his ear.

With Kai in place, Conryu went to create a distraction. The trick was to have it be serious enough to set off the alarms, but not have anyone realize it was him doing it. As he left the lab and flew up into the sky, Conryu settled on a few lightning strikes. But first he'd need a storm.

At about five thousand feet, he stepped out of the library, invisible of course, and started spinning the staff over his head. Dark clouds quickly gathered followed by rumbles of thunder. He let the storm build, quickly, but not too quickly. Just a pop-up late summer storm, nothing extraordinary.

When his storm had grown to his satisfaction, Conryu nudged the electrical current, building it up and guiding the energy. The first bolt hit a car in the nearly empty parking lot and blew it to smithereens. The next two crashed into the building's wards, lighting them up but doing no harm. Heavy rain and winds came next.

Five minutes after the storm began, Kai's head appeared beside him. "It's done, Chosen."

"Good. Let's go collect my mom and head to the Academy. I think she, Maria, and Dean Blane need to have a long talk."

## CHAPTER 15

Merik wasn't sure how long he'd been in Atlantis. There was no night or day, just a steady light that seemed to come from everywhere without a definite source. He hadn't eaten since he arrived, yet he felt no hunger. Tanidel said it was a function of the city's magic. They existed outside of the normal time stream, so thirst, hunger and aging were basically suspended. Boredom, unfortunately, was still an issue.

After Tanidel had led him to a suite larger than his house, fully decorated with crystal furniture, she left him to his own devices. The survivors hadn't offered to speak with him again. The more he thought about it, the more that first meeting felt like they were just going through the motions. Merik had done what they needed him to and now he was cast aside, his services no longer required.

That was how he felt at least. Since he knew nothing about how their crystal magic worked, he had little to offer in the way of help in preparing for the city's return. Surely when they got back, he would have an important role to play.

A powerful vibration ran through the room, raising goosebumps on the back of his arm. Merik hopped out of his hard crystal chair and walked toward the area of the wall where the door appeared. At least it appeared for Tanidel, he had no actual idea how to get out of the room. Merik did his best not to think of it as a prison cell.

Ten feet from the entrance, the wall opened revealing Tanidel outside.

"I felt something strange," Merik said.

"We have reached the edge of the human realm. The others are preparing to make the transition. We all wanted you to be there to witness our return. Come with me."

He fell in beside her and they walked out of the tower. She led him toward the center of the city.

As they walked Merik said, "I thought you'd forgotten about me."

"I apologize for that. The preparations for our return have taken every moment. Even with the path marked, shifting an object the size of the city is no easy feat."

Her polite apology and explanation made his fears seem petty. Of course they were focused on other things. "It's okay. I just wish you had cable or something."

"Cable?"

Right, of course they knew nothing about television. "Did you have some way to watch the world during your exile?"

"We could open portals for a short time, but it took so much energy and the information gained was largely useless, so we abandoned the effort ages ago."

"Man, are you all going to be in for a surprise. The world has gone through some serious changes since you left."

"Yes, I saw many of them in your memories when our minds were linked. It should prove interesting. Here we are."

Tanidel had led him to a massive red crystal. It towered

over the eleven figures standing in a circle around it. The crystal was the same color as the key he'd found and his allies used to recall the city.

"Welcome to the heart of Atlantis," Tanidel said. "Keep a few feet back while we complete the ritual."

She stepped into the gap in their circle and took the hands of the Atlanteans to her left and right. The twelve of them raised their silent gazes to the sky and their bodies began to glow. The red crystal picked up the light and shaded everything crimson.

A vibration ran through Merik.

It grew in intensity until he feared he might be rattled to pieces.

When his teeth were on the verge of popping out of his head it stopped.

A startled squawk drew his attention upward. White clouds dotted the clear blue sky and a single seagull glided away from the towers.

They were back at last.

The survivors broke their circle and moved his way. If they were tired their crystal bodies gave no indication. No matter what they never seemed to change. If he was honest it gave him the creeps; looking at their blank facial expressions was like staring at a mask, he couldn't get a read on their intentions.

"What happens now?" Merik asked.

"The ancestors of Lemuria will have sensed our return," one of the men said. "The city is protected from their magic as are we. Still, we must move quickly before they can attempt to isolate us. The religious fanatics that hate wizards, they will be our natural allies. Merik, you will introduce three of us to their leader. The rest of us will prepare our weapons for the coming war. Go quickly."

Tanidel took the lead, setting a brisk pace toward the eastern edge of the city. The two men – he really needed to make up names for them – fell in behind her, leaving Merik to bring up the rear. He had no idea where they were going, or where the city was for that matter. He assumed somewhere off the coast of the Kingdom of the Isles near Stonehenge, given that was where the tether was, but for all he knew they could have appeared anywhere on the planet.

Ten minutes later they reached the edge of the city. Merik had expected to see the ocean, not a sheer cliff. He looked over and about three hundred feet below them saw the white caps of the waves.

"I didn't know Atlantis was a flying city," he said.

"It wasn't originally," Tanidel said. "It was the capital city of a large island nation. That island is long gone now. We transformed a number of the crystal towers into lift generators. The city can't fly but does levitate and we can generate a field that makes us invisible to anyone nearby. It even hides us from magical detection."

The two men, Larry and Curly, Merik decided to call them, were crouched a few feet away, their hands touching the crystal at the edge of the cliff. As Merik watched, a flat-bottomed boat slowly took shape.

"It's going to take a long time to row to the archbishop's palace."

"Do you see any oars?" Tanidel asked. "This boat can fly."

After three conversations with the leader of the Ministry of Magic, it was clear to Sienna that Jemma wasn't taking her warnings seriously. Sienna rolled over on her back and stared up at the white ceiling. The healing and rest had done wonders to restore her strength. It was time to get out of here and get back to her mission.

What that mission was now, she was less certain. Her sense of time was scrambled, but Atlantis's return had to be imminent. No one knew more about the enemy than she did, though Sienna knew little enough. She should be out searching for a way to stop them, not lying around dressed in a paper gown.

She rolled out of bed and stood on the cool tile. It was time to go. But first clothes.

There was a tall, narrow closet just inside the door. Maybe she could find something useful in there. There were some pants made out of rough blue cloth nearly as flimsy as her gown. She pulled them on anyway and tucked the gown in around them. If anyone saw her on the street, they'd think she escaped from a mental institute. Fortunately, Sienna didn't intend to travel by foot.

She concentrated, trying to slip into the realm of wind. No portal formed. As she feared, some ward prevented portals from opening in the building. A perfectly reasonable precaution for a place like this.

Before she could step into the hall, the door opened and her nurse came in. The woman in white gave her outfit one look and said, "Going somewhere?"

"Yes. I thank you for healing my wounds, but I have lingered here far too long. If you would return my sword, I will be on my way."

"I'm not sure where your sword is, but I do know the director wouldn't approve of you leaving. Why don't you lie back down and I'll go find her?"

"Unless I'm a prisoner, I'm leaving, with or without my sword."

Sienna took a step toward the door, but the nurse didn't

budge. She'd never fought a fellow wizard before, but there was a first time for everything.

"Step aside, please. I have no wish to harm you."

"I tried to be nice about this, but my orders are not to let you out of this room. Ahh!" The nurse crumpled to her knees.

A jagged lance of pain ran through Sienna's head. It was so much stronger than her previous encounters with Atlantean magic that she had no doubt what it meant. Atlantis had returned.

As quick as it came the pain vanished.

Before she could recover, Sienna kicked the nurse in the side of the head. She went limp.

Sienna started to step over the body then thought better of it. The nurse wasn't much shorter than her. A uniform would attract much less attention than her gown and pants. A few minutes of work found Sienna dressed in the nurse's white robe and the nurse tucked up under the covers of Sienna's bed.

She stepped out into the hall and turned right, looking for an exit sign. There had to be a door somewhere around here. A few feet away was a semicircular table covered with computers and phones. Another woman in white manned the station. She was massaging her temples. The appearance of Atlantis would have struck wizards all over the world. Before the nurse could glance her way, Sienna walked to her left.

The infirmary wasn't huge and she quickly spotted the exit. Unfortunately, the door had a magical pad beside it. Sienna grabbed the handle, but as she feared it was locked. The pad had to be what activated the lock, but she had no idea how to use it. She glanced out the little window and spotted a figure in a black robe headed toward her.

Jemma was coming with more questions. Sienna had no more time to waste. She could sense how powerful the woman in black was. If she had to fight her way out, she was doomed before the first spell was cast.

Sienna darted back to the nearest room and shoved the door open. It was exactly the same as her room. Smashing the heavy glass of the window wouldn't be easy, but it was her only way out.

She put her hand to the window and cast, "Icy spirits of the north, grant me your blessing. Frozen Burst!"

Frost creeped out, covering the window until it was frosted over. Sienna grabbed the guest chair and hurled it at the pane.

The window shattered.

She climbed up on the ledge just as the door opened behind her.

"Stop!" Jemma shouted.

There was no magic behind the command.

Sienna leapt.

They were only five stories up, but that was plenty of time for her to shift into the realm of wind. Safe in the spirit's realm, for the moment at least, she flew as far and as fast as she could away from the Ministry.

During their conversations, Jemma thought she was learning from Sienna, but Sienna had learned a thing or two as well. The most important of which was the name of the foremost expert on the strongest wizard in the world. She needed to speak to her old friend Angus.

If anyone could help her stop Atlantis, it was Conryu Koda.

---

Jemma sat at her desk, hardly able to contain her anger. Somehow, her people had allowed the only person that could offer any explanation for the strange surge of energy to escape. Granted they weren't at their best. Jemma's head was still throbbing after that spike of pain. She refused to believe it was a coincidence. Whatever happened had to have something to do with this Atlantis business.

She ground her teeth. Atlantis. There was no way she could deny the possibility, however unlikely it appeared. There was a knock on her door and Celia stuck her head in. "Wind wizards report no sign of her and the spirits aren't talking. What do you want to do?"

"Call them back. I'm sure she's long gone by now."

Celia nodded and ducked back out. If the spirits refused to tell her people where Sienna had gone, it meant she had their blessing for whatever she was doing. That also implied that Jemma shouldn't interfere. One of the unspoken rules of wizardry was that when the spirits chose a side, you respected that.

Politics, alas, had different rules. She was ready to make her report to the crown. Assuming the king didn't laugh her out of her post, she'd have to explain how she let Sienna escape. Not a conversation she was looking forward to.

Another knock drew a groan. "Not now, Celia."

The door opened anyway. A man she didn't recognize stood in her doorway. He was dressed in a blue uniform and clutched a beret in his left hand. "Beg pardon, ma'am, but I was sent over by the Royal Air Force. Our weather stations recorded some strange readings a few minutes ago and they wanted the opinion of the Ministry about whether it was a magical phenomenon. The lass at the front desk sent me to ask you."

The last thing she needed was an interdepartmental consultation. Wait. "Do you have the exact time?"

He pulled a notepad out of his back pocket. "Two twenty-three and fifteen seconds."

Jemma checked the clock on her desk. That was exactly

when the first instant of pain stabbed every wizard she'd spoken to in the head.

She leapt to her feet. "Take me to whoever recorded those readings."

Jemma and her new companion made the short walk from the Ministry Building to military headquarters three blocks down the street. The Royal Air Force operated out of an ugly, square building six stories tall and topped with all manner of antennas and dishes. In addition to protecting the Kingdom from any airborne threat, the RAF also tracked the weather to as precise a degree as possible. She suspected they spent more time on that than they did flying considering no enemy had attacked the island from the air in a century. At least no enemy the RAF had a hope of defeating.

The young man held the door for Jemma then guided her through a nearly empty waiting room to an elevator. They rode up to the top floor in silence. She got the distinct impression that she intimidated him. Jemma was used to that reaction. She intimidated pretty much everyone she met for the first time.

The bell chimed and they stepped out into a hallway running left and right. Her guide turned right and made the brief walk to a closed door. He rapped twice and opened it.

Behind a desk covered with computer monitors sat a man with an iron-gray beard dressed in a blue uniform decorated with a dozen medals. He stood when she entered and they shook hands. His gaze was steady and grip firm. Nice to see someone at the RAF had some steel in them.

"When I sent off for a consultant," the officer said in a thick Scottish accent. "I didn't think the bloody idiot would bring the head of the Ministry back with him. Colonel Cable at your service, ma'am. Won't you sit?"

Jemma sat in one of the chairs facing his desk. Cable waved his subordinate off and the door closed a moment later.

"Seeing as how you've come yourself; I assume calling for help was a good decision. Truth is I've never seen a sudden burst of wind like this. Not to mention a crack of thunder that came out of nowhere on a perfect sunny day. If it isn't magic, then I don't know."

"Can you show me exactly where the readings were recorded?" Jemma asked.

"Sure can." Cable spun one of his three monitors so she could see it then punched a command into his keyboard. "There you are."

A map of the island appeared along with the surrounding water. A flashing red light indicated the anomaly's location. It was only a few miles away from Stonehenge. A large mass appearing suddenly would certainly explain both the wind and the thunder. She needed to be sure.

"Do you have any surveillance aircraft available?"

"None in the air, but we can scramble one in fifteen minutes."

"Does your place have room for a passenger?"

"Sure, will you send one of your people over?"

"I'm going myself."

## CHAPTER 16

Conryu, his mother, Prime, and Kai arrived at the Academy less than an hour after his conversation with Connel. To say his mother had been excited to hear there was another, different crystal would be putting it mildly. He hadn't seen her so worked up in a while. They left one library and entered another. Most of the students were still asleep and the library was empty. That suited him fine. The fewer people that knew they were there the better.

While Kai went to fetch Maria and Dean Blane, Conryu and his mother settled in to wait.

"Did you really mail the magic-negating crystal to the Ministry of Magic in London?" his mother asked.

"Sure, why not? You said you guys got it by mail. It's not like I can send it magically. Honestly, those things are a bloody nuisance."

"They were designed to be, at least to wizards. I'm sorry the soldiers came after you with them."

"No need to apologize, Mom. You didn't send them." Conryu licked his lips. There was never going to be a better time to bring this up. In fact, he'd waited too long as it was. "Have you been doing okay, since Dad died? I know I haven't been around as much as I should have."

"I miss him, terribly." Her voice broke along with Conryu's heart. "But I'm okay. One day at a time, right? I've got my work which helps a lot. Though my focus appears to have blinded me to what was really happening. And don't worry for a second about not being with me. I understand why you couldn't be. We're together now. That's what counts."

He reached out and took her hand. "I love you, Mom."

"I love you too, dear."

Kai appeared a moment later. "They are coming, Chosen."

Conryu gave his mother's hand a final squeeze and stood just as the library door opened. Maria and Dean Blane entered and hurried over to the table. Introductions were made and Maria hugged his mother.

Dean Blane placed the clear crystal on the table. "Here it is."

"And this one can detect wizard potential by testing blood?" His mother closed her eyes and placed a finger on the crystal. "No vibration. Maybe it only happens when the crystal's power activates. That would make sense. The gray one was constantly active and so vibrated constantly."

She went on muttering to herself seeming blissfully unaware that there was anyone else in the room.

Dean Blane motioned him off to one side. "Did you get a stabbing pain in your head a little while ago?"

"No. Why, what happened?"

"I don't know," Dean Blane said. "It hit everyone at the same time. Woke many of the girls out of a dead sleep. I can't believe you didn't feel it."

"Whatever it was probably happened when we were in the library. Being in another dimension might have protected us. Were there any lingering effects?"

"No, it only lasted a few seconds." Dean Blane shook her youthful head. "I've never experienced anything like it. I reached out to some friends in other parts of the Alliance and they felt it too."

Conryu sighed. Another mystery, just what they needed.

"Could I trouble someone for some blood?" his mother asked.

Before Conryu could reply, Kai drew her sword, touched her thumb to the blade, and let a few drops of blood fall on the crystal. It absorbed the blood and turned pitch black. It worked the way they expected at least.

His mother touched the crystal again, a look of intense focus scrunching up her face. After a few seconds she smiled. "It's vibrating! I knew it! The vibration is softer than the gray crystals, but definitely there. The strength must vary depending on the power of the effect it's trying to create."

"Magic based on vibrations?" Dean Blane said. "I've never even considered such a thing."

"Can we counter the vibrations?" Conryu asked. "If there are more of those anti-magic crystals lying around it would be nice if we had a way of negating their effect."

Mom got that faraway look she got when she was deep in thought. "I suppose if one frequency causes an effect, an inverse vibration should negate it. You'd need something to generate the vibrations, some way to calibrate them so they matched the precise pitch you needed, and a way to direct them. The crystals are designed to do what they do. There's some sort of internal energy source that powers the vibrations."

"What sort of energy source?" Maria asked.

"I wish I knew," his mother said.

"Why don't you just smash the crystal and see what's inside?" Prime said.

Everyone faced the demon book and somehow Prime managed to look nervous.

Conryu grinned. That wasn't a terrible idea. "Anyone got a hammer?"

"If we smash it, we won't have anything else to experiment on," Dean Blane said.

"Are there more experiments you want to run?" Conryu asked.

Dean Blane looked at Maria who shrugged. "Now that you ask, I can't really think of anything we haven't tried. Did you want to try anything else, Mrs. Koda?"

"No, I don't think so. Connel and I have been testing the one at the lab for months. We'd run into a wall. Neither of us really considered damaging such a unique artifact, but if we're to figure it out, I see no other option."

"Chosen?" Kai had her sword out and ready.

"Go ahead, Kai, but be careful. Mom, get behind me." When his mother had moved to a safe position, he conjured an invisible wall in front of everyone and nodded to Kai.

She brought the hilt of her sword down squarely on the now-black crystal.

It shattered into dozens of pieces, the darkness vanishing instantly.

He lowered his barrier and everyone hurried to look over the pieces. His mother pushed the pieces around, looking each one over as she did. Dean Blane and Maria both cast detection spells.

Conryu was content to let those who knew what they were doing work. Complex analysis wasn't his strong suit and he knew it.

Five minutes after Kai shattered the crystal, a phone rang. Dean Blane reached into the robe and pulled out a simple flip phone. Conryu frowned at her. Cell phones were supposed to be banned at the Academy.

She noticed his expression and shrugged. "It's for emergencies. Hello?"

Dean Blane listened for a minute then said, "And you only thought to mention this now? Don't give me that bureaucratic bullshit. Crazy or not, she clearly knew about the crystals. Atlantis, seriously? And what is that noise? Why are you in a plane and not flying on your own? What? Fine, call me back when you know something more."

"Trouble?" Conryu asked.

Dean Blane closed her phone and tucked it away. "That was Jemma. She captured a woman near Stonehenge who claims the crystal magic comes from Atlantis, that the city is returning, and they are going to do away with all wizards."

"Sounds like trouble to me," Conryu said.

꒟

Jemma pocketed her phone and grimaced. She'd expected Dean Blane to be annoyed with her; if the shoe had been on the other foot, she would have been annoyed as well. Fortunately, the roar of the spy plane's engines made it difficult to talk for long, though she was certain the next time they spoke face to face, Jemma was going to get an earful.

For now, she needed to focus on the matter at hand. The back of the plane wasn't designed for passengers. The two pilots rode up front and masses of computer equipment filled the fuselage. She wiped sweat from her brow. The bloody things put out a ton of heat.

There were no windows or chairs, so she was forced to wedge herself between two cabinets filled with hard disks. The technicians had also rigged her up a high definition monitor so she could see what was outside. Right now, only clouds were visible.

"Approaching the target coordinates, ma'am," one of the pilots announced over the intercom.

Jemma muttered a detection spell, but if they were dealing with crystal magic, she doubted she'd be able to sense anything. The plane banked as they made a slow circle around the place where the RAF picked up the strange readings.

There was nothing out there but more clouds.

When they'd completed a full circle, the pilot said. "We've completed our sweep. Do we return or remain on station?"

The plane had a huge fuel tank and was more than capable of circling an area for hours. Jemma had no desire to spend hours looking at the empty sky. Still, she had to be sure.

"One more pass if you please," she said.

As they banked, Jemma watched the screen even more carefully. Halfway through the circuit, a gull banked through the area, weaving its way in a zigzagging path through the sky. Why would it fly that way if there was nothing out there?

"Is this plane armed?" Jemma asked.

"No, ma'am," the pilot said. "We do have defensive flares."

"That will do. Did you see that gull fly through the target area?"

There was a long pause. "Yes, we see it on the recording."

"I want you to climb, fly over that precise area, and disperse your flares. Track their trajectory with the cameras. I want to know if they hit anything."

"You think there's something invisible out there?" the pilot asked. "Do I need to call in a fighter escort?"

"Let's confirm that something's there before we make fools of ourselves."

"Understood."

The plane climbed and banked.

Jemma kept her eyes glued to the screen.

There was a series of rapid pops, like fireworks going off, then the flares fell through her field of view. The bright dots fell slowly.

Come on, I know you're hiding here somewhere.

One of the flares shifted right as if it hit something. A second one further on did the same.

"Are you seeing this, ma'am?" the pilot asked.

"I see it. Log the recording and get us out of here."

"Roger."

Before the plane could bank, a massive shimmer filled the air. When it vanished an entire crystal city appeared below them. Dozens of towers that looked like they were made of glass jutted into the air.

One of the towers began to glow.

"Get us out of here now!" Jemma shouted.

Too late.

A beam of crimson light shot out and sliced the plane in half between her and the cockpit.

Jemma cast the fastest flying spell of her life and shot through the debris toward the tumbling cockpit. The pilots didn't have ejection seats in a plane like this. She had to reach them before they hit the rapidly approaching water.

She dove, casting a protective spell as she went.

Jagged pieces of metal broke off the cockpit and hurtled toward her. They pinged off her shield and she kept going.

When she reached the cockpit, both pilots had their belts off.

She grabbed them and chanted.

The crystal tower was glowing again.

Jemma opened a portal to the realm of wind.

The three of them fell through it an instant before the tower could fire.

Floating in the swirling void, Jemma blew out a long sigh. They'd survived for the moment.

"What the bloody hell was that?" one of the pilots asked.

"Atlantis," Jemma said, not caring if she sounded mad. Everything Sienna said was true. The city had returned.

## CHAPTER 17

Merik had done some crazy things since learning of his heritage but flying at break-neck speed in a crystal rowboat went right to the top of the list. They were so low he could have reached out and touched the treetops. It was unlikely the church had a high-tech anti-aircraft system or even one that would have been able to detect them given their size and lack of an engine, but Tanidel and her comrades weren't taking any chances. Merik kept his opinions to himself, but he figured the biggest danger was someone looking up, seeing them, and calling the church.

"Is that it?" Tanidel asked.

Merik squinted. In the distance, a huge white marble palace filled the horizon. It had to be at least thirty thousand square feet with hundreds of acres of lawns and parks surrounding it. No vow of poverty for the archbishop, that was certain. If the extravagance bothered anyone, they were smart enough to keep quiet or risk getting a visit from the inquisition.

Tiny figures patrolled the grounds. He assumed those were

guards assigned to protect the archbishop from his adoring followers.

"That's it," Merik said. "Any thoughts on how we land without getting shot?"

"Their weapons are no threat to us," Curly said. "Even you can withstand a few bullets without fear."

Just because he could didn't mean Merik was eager to prove it. "This place has to have a helipad. I don't see one on the grounds so that means it's probably on the roof. Why don't we land there and work our way down?"

"Avoiding confrontation would be prudent," Tanidel said.

"Very well." Curly didn't seem overly interested in avoiding a confrontation.

The boat slowed as they got closer. Any moment Merik expected bullets to start pinging off the hull. None of the guards even looked up as they passed overhead. He frowned. There was some magic going that he didn't grasp. Merik almost asked about it but didn't want to draw attention by speaking.

The crystal boat landed in the middle of a circle marked with an H. If the helicopter wasn't here, then the archbishop might not be either. That could be a problem, though one easily solved with a few questions in the right ear.

When they had all gotten out, Larry and Curly led the way to a door that went inside. The handle didn't budge when Larry grabbed it. His right arm glowed and he reared back, ripping the door off its hinges, and tossing it aside.

Merik winced. So much for stealth.

There was a small landing inside the door and a set of stairs leading to the top floor. Larry took the lead, his crystal feet clattering on the steel stairs like cymbals crashing. A stampede of cattle would have been quieter.

At the bottom of the steps was another door, this one

unlocked. Larry pulled it open and took a bullet to his crystal face. It ricocheted off without leaving a mark.

"Remain here," Larry said.

He and Curly stepped out into the hall. The clatter of machine guns filled the air.

"Don't worry," Tanidel said. "Our crystal bodies are very sturdy. They will be fine."

Merik was less worried about Larry and Curly than he was the guards. If they wanted to make an alliance with the archbishop, killing his minions wasn't the best way to introduce themselves.

Soon enough the hall fell silent. Tanidel pushed the door open and Merik followed her out into the hall expecting to find bodies torn to pieces. Instead he found a group of six men in bulletproof vests and military fatigues lying on the floor, still breathing, and reasonably intact. Thank heaven they had some notion of restraint.

"The archbishop has been moved to somewhere called a secure room," Larry said. "We have the location."

The secure room was in the palace basement. They ran into three more armed groups which Larry and Curly dealt with as easily as the first. They were like monsters from a horror movie come to life. No matter what the guards tried it had no effect on their crystal bodies. Merik was beginning to think that a dozen Atlanteans might be enough to defeat the world's wizards after all.

A heavy armored door protected the secure room. However strong they were, Merik doubted Larry and Curly would be able to rip it off its hinges like they had every other door so far. In fact, they didn't even try. Larry punched a sequence of numbers into a keypad and the door swung open on its own.

"How did they know that?" Merik asked.

"I'm sure they extracted it from one of the guards' minds like they did the room's location," Tanidel said. "Who are Larry and Curly?"

Merik grinned. "We're connected, aren't we? I'd forgotten. They were characters on an old tv show I watched as a kid. I needed some way to think of your friends since they didn't have names of their own. Those just popped into my head. If you could read that, couldn't you read the memory as well?"

"Our connection only allows me to see your surface thoughts. Anything deeper would require a probe and might damage your mind."

During their brief conversation, Larry had gone in and pulled an old man in white robes out into the hall. He was decorated with so much gold jewelry it was a wonder he could walk under all that weight.

The archbishop's gaze latched onto Merik the way a drowning man's might on a piece of driftwood. "Please, whatever you want is yours, only ask."

"Archbishop, I apologize for our methods in getting in touch with you. I had hoped that a bishop of my acquaintance could handle the introductions, but he was killed without mercy by a wizard," Merik said. "None of your followers have been permanently harmed and neither shall you be. You see, we have come in search of allies. My companions and I are the sworn enemy of wizards. When they asked me to advise them as to who would be their greatest friend in a war against the wizards of the world, I said without hesitation that they should seek out the True Face of God."

The archbishop slowly relaxed under the combination of reassurance and compliments. "If you are the enemy of those godless monstrosities then we will be brothers for sure. What do you propose?"

Merik glanced at Tanidel. He didn't actually know the survivors' plans for the war.

She said, "We have the means to negate their magic, but we lack numbers. If you provide soldiers, we will protect them from the enemy's magic."

"If you can stop their cursed sorcery, then you truly are angels come from Heaven. Nothing would make my people happier than slaughtering every one of the cursed wizards."

"You should gather them for a blessing and to announce the crusade," Larry said. "If you introduce us as friends, your followers won't be afraid."

"Certainly, certainly. I can hardly contain my joy at the prospect."

"How long will it take to gather your followers?" Curly asked.

"A few days. Never fear, we have a plan for just such an occasion. I will send out the announcement at once." The archbishop bustled away toward the stairs with Larry and Curly behind him.

Tanidel gently touched his shoulder. "Once again you have proven your worth to your people. You handled him brilliantly."

"I was a salesman; this was just another sort of sale. I'm pleased I could be of use."

Merik smiled as they followed the others upstairs. It finally felt like they were accomplishing something.

Angus tossed aside a book on theories of ancient Egyptian magic, adding it to the heap of books beside his desk. He blew out a sigh. Glad as he was to be back home with all his bits intact, the loss of Atlantis as a research subject had taken the wind out of his sails. There were so many great myths out there that might have some truth to them, but whenever he tried to dig into one his mind started drifting back to the young woman that nearly killed him and the stolen crystal. It was too delicious a mystery to just let go. On the other hand, he had no desire to end up on the wrong side of her sword again.

He pushed away from his desk. A cup of tea would be just the thing to settle his churning mind and get him focused. That monograph on the wendigo sounded interesting. Then again, Angus didn't especially like the cold and they all apparently lived in the northern mountains. Maybe the weird zombies that washed up in Florida would be a better subject.

His battered tea kettle went on the stove to boil while he dug out a cup and infuser. No damn tea bags for him, thank you very much. They were an abomination designed for those too lazy to make a proper cup of tea. He'd just set a tiny pitcher of cream on the kitchen table when his doorbell rang.

Angus wasn't expecting company. In fact, he seldom got company beyond the occasional reporter wanting a comment on Conryu's departure from the Alliance. Giving one of those fair-weather fans a good bawling out was just what he needed to clear his thoughts.

Eager for the confrontation, he shuffled out of the kitchen, through his modest front room, to the door. He didn't bother looking out the peep hole. His eyesight was bad enough that all he ever saw was a blur anyway. He unlocked the door and yanked it open, ready for an argument, only to find himself facing the young lady that drove him away from Stonehenge, minus the sword.

"Professor McDoogle," she said. "I require your aid."

Fully taken aback by both her presence and request, he

could only stare until the whistling of his kettle shook him out of his stupor. "Would you like to discuss it over a cup of tea?"

He was surprised again when she said, "A cup of tea would be nice, thank you."

Angus stepped aside and ushered her in. He led the way back to the kitchen where he took the kettle off and poured them both cups. With the herbs steeping he asked, "How may I be of assistance? In truth I had no expectation of ever seeing you again after we parted ways."

"Nor did I of seeing you, but circumstances have changed. You see, your successor was a soldier and he had friends. Despite my best efforts, he succeeded in returning Atlantis to this realm. It's a battle now. Either we stop them, or every wizard will die."

Angus licked his lips. This was way outside of his expertise. "How, exactly, did you think I could help?"

"While I am a skilled combatant, my magical power is limited. I need the aid of a powerful wizard. It is my understanding that you know the strongest. I require an introduction to Conryu Koda."

He winced. While he was an expert on Conryu and the legends of Merlin, it wasn't like they were friends. In fact, Conryu rather disliked him.

The herbs were finished and he took the infusers to the sink. He returned and sat across from her. "Conryu and I aren't friends. In fact, I have no idea where to find him. The last rumor I heard had him living on one of the floating islands. How he got on to one I have no idea. I fear you've come all this way for nothing."

She gave him a hard look over the rim of her cup and for a moment Angus forgot all about the delightful aroma filling the kitchen and he was back at Stonehenge with her sword at his throat.

"You may not know exactly where he is, but you do know how to find him. Someone has a way to contact him. Who would it be?"

Several immediately came to mind, but he was only sure about one. "His mother would know. I can take you to their apartment. Say, what is your name, anyway?"

"Sienna." She took a sip and her expression softened. "This is excellent tea. Perhaps you can make some for Conryu's mother when we arrive."

## CHAPTER 18

Merik could hardly believe how quickly the cultists arrived from all over the country. They came by car, by bus, and in one bishop's case, by helicopter. Hundreds of them were now gathered in neat rows facing the palace. He and the other Atlanteans were keeping out of sight for now. The archbishop was supposed to introduce them as avatars of God's wrath or something equally stupid.

He stepped away from the window and shook his head. The foolishness of the average person never ceased to amaze him. He'd often marveled at it while dealing with his clients, how easy they were to manipulate if you just told them what they wanted to hear.

Tanidel was standing behind him when he turned around. Merik nearly leapt out of his skin. "I didn't realize you were that stealthy."

"I'm not, you were distracted. The others are preparing the archbishop for his big moment. I wanted to thank you again for everything you've done for us. I know my fellows can seem hard and distant, but it's only because they're focused on the mission. We have already lost once to the Lemurians; our only hope of defeating them lies in quick, decisive action. I'm sure they will show you the proper appreciation when the time comes."

"Your thanks are enough. What happens after the blessing? Where will we strike first?"

"The first blow is already in the works. It is more symbolic than strategic, but it will happen soon. And when it does, the world will take notice."

"Have you spoken to the others?" Merik asked.

"I don't need to. A single vibration connects us all. Our minds are fully open to each other. Your crystal connects you to us, but it isn't the same. For us to speak mind to mind I must focus and create a link. With the others, it's like we're each pieces of a larger whole."

"Sounds… strange."

"It would be for you, but we have spent thousands of years getting used to it. I can't imagine what it would be like for one of them to go silent."

"What about—"

She silenced him with a raised hand. After a moment she said, "The time for the blessing has arrived. We should join the others."

Merik was going to ask about others with the blood of Atlantis, but it could wait. They walked down marble halls and up a flight of steps to a balcony overlooking the assembled cultists. Larry and Curly arrived with the archbishop seconds after them. The old man stood straight and proud in his gaudy official robes. He looked far better than when they'd found him hiding in his dark hole in the basement. He must have psyched himself up for his speech.

"Your followers are waiting," Larry said.

The archbishop nodded and stepped out on the balcony. The roar from below seemed to shake the palace. The madmen really did worship their leader. Merik had always assumed most of them paid lip service to the church as they climbed the ladder. It seemed he had underestimated the power of their faith.

"My children." The archbishop's voice carried easily to his flock who had fallen into rapt silence. "The time for the great crusade we have long awaited is here."

An even bigger cheer went up.

When it died down, he continued. "God has sent us champions to lead the faithful to victory. Behold the crystal angels!"

Larry and Curly stepped out on cue to thunderous applause.

"Should we join them?" Merik asked.

"No, one at each of his shoulders is more dramatic."

"Lower your heads in prayer and prepare to receive my blessing." Using some magic Merik didn't understand, Larry and Curly carried the archbishop into the air and down to his waiting followers.

Merik took a step closer to get a better look. Larry held a bowl and as they walked along the rows, the archbishop dipped his thumb into the bowl and drew a cross on each person's forehead. It took several hours, but finally he marked the last person, a boy not more than sixteen.

"What now?" Merik asked.

"Watch," Tanidel said. "Watch and see the birth of an army."

Merik didn't care for the sudden fervor in her voice, but he turned to see what would happen next.

"Raise your eyes, my children," the archbishop said.

Everyone looked up and Curly slapped his hands together once. A high, pure tone rang out over the assembly. For a moment Merik thought it was symbolism, then the people began to collapse. One by one they fell to their knees. Crystals sprang from their foreheads and spread quickly, covering first their faces then heads and soon their whole bodies.

When the process was complete, everyone, including the archbishop himself, had been transformed into crystal figures, similar to and yet different from Tanidel and the other Atlanteans. The cultists' forms were jagged and covered with spikes. They had no real faces, only glowing slits where their eyes had been.

They were a nightmare come to life.

"What have you done to them?" Merik asked.

"Turned them into something useful. Flesh and blood are weak. These crystal soldiers are immune to magic, resistant to most forms of damage, and absolutely obedient to our orders. With this force we will capture more towns and cities where we will make more soldiers and on and on until the world is ours."

This wasn't what he'd expected at all.

"I sense your fear," Tanidel said. "Be at ease. You are one of us. Your future is your own to choose. Eternal life in a crystal body or a mortal life in your current body. For all that you have done, you may rest assured that we will honor your choice."

"Are you going to change everyone?" Merik asked. "I thought you only wanted to eliminate the wizards."

"We do want to eliminate the wizards and we will, but when every living wizard is dead, more may be born. Only by getting rid of all the people will the scourge of wizards end. After all, once all the people are dead, there will be no one left for the spirits to bless. Come, the others are ready for us."

Merik hesitated then fell in behind her. After all, what choice did he have?

There was a room in the Academy that Conryu hadn't even known existed. All manner of scientific gadgets covered shelves and workbenches. The moment his mother saw it, she settled in and got to work, a happy smile on her face. He was content to leave her with Maria and Dean Blane while he retreated to the library and Kai joined the ninjas on guard duty.

He had friends at the Academy – he wanted to have a chat with Kelsie, see how she was managing in her final year – but for now he didn't want to advertise his presence. He'd been here long enough that the teachers and stronger students should have sensed him. Hopefully none of them would do anything foolish like letting the army know he was here.

He had a book in front of him filled with complex diagrams and incantations, most of which made little sense and reminded him again why he hated research.

He looked over at Prime. "You've been awfully quiet lately. Usually you're full of advice. What gives?"

"When I try to comment on your predicament, I find myself unable to speak," Prime said. "I believe the Reaper's injunction affects me despite my altered form. I am sorry, Master."

Conryu blew out a sigh and closed his book. He needed to make contact with the Reaper and find out once and for all what he was hiding. If a regular demon couldn't tell him what he wanted to know, he'd go right to the top. There was no way he could get this business sorted out with his hands tied behind his back.

"A confrontation with the Reaper might not be the best idea," Prime said. "He's not known for his tolerance of people questioning his commands."

"If you have a better idea, I'm all ears."

Prime remained silent which was a statement all on its own.

Conryu stood. Bad idea or not, he needed information and knew of nowhere else to get it. He was about to leave the library and open a Hell gate when a faint buzzing appeared in the back of his mind. It came from Maria's rune stone. Hopefully she and his mother had learned something.

The library door opened into the technology workshop. Everyone was gathered around an old flat-screen tv in the far-left corner. They stared at it with such intensity no one seemed to have noticed he arrived.

"What's going on?" he asked.

Maria dragged her gaze away from the tv. "One of the floating islands just fell on Madagascar."

He took a moment to process that. "How?"

"No one seems to know, at least not yet," Dean Blane said. "The island that fell is back in the air and has resumed its regular course. It missed all the major towns. In fact, no one was hurt by the island itself, though some were injured in the earthquake that followed. Everyone on the news is baffled. As am I for that matter."

"What's the island's course?" Conryu asked. "Will it pass over any other inhabited area soon?"

"Not for a few days," his mother said. "The island has moved out over the ocean and is headed toward India. Based on estimates it will take two to three days to reach the mainland. A day after that it will pass over Mumbai."

"If it falls there," Conryu said. "It'll kill millions. Kai!"

The ninja appeared beside him. "Chosen?"

"We're taking a trip."

"Wait," Maria said. "Whatever disrupted the island's magic could disrupt yours as well. It's too dangerous."

"If the island is back in the air then its barrier must be up as well. If that's the case, no one else can get in. I'm not going to stand around and do nothing when that damn thing might fall on a city." The library door appeared at his mental command. "I'll be careful. You guys focus on finding a way to deal with those crystals."

She looked like she wanted to argue some more, but he entered the library before she had a chance. He loved Maria and knew she was right about the danger, but he couldn't let that stop him from doing what he had to.

Jemma had just completed her report to the king. Sitting on his golden throne with a purple robe of office wrapped around him like a blanket, he looked tired and sunk in rather than regal. The last few months had taken a toll, on all of them, but on him the most. The crown looked like it weighed a hundred pounds.

At least he took the news of a mythical city floating just off the Kingdom's coast with surprising calm. Perhaps after half the Kingdom's cities were flattened by another figure from virtual myth only months ago, he'd become numb to the bizarre. Either way, she was relieved to find him in full possession of his faculties. A panicked king would do no one any good.

Just to prove turnabout was fair play, he had informed her that one of the floating islands had fallen out of the sky and crushed a massive area of Madagascar and no one yet knew why. A team had been dispatched, but they had little hope of finding a way through the island's barrier. It was another mess she didn't need, but at least it was a faraway one, for now at least.

After their briefing, the two of them descended to the palace command center, a room filled with computers and monitors, and connected to the Kingdom's many outposts and satellites. From here they could monitor events all over the world in nearly real time. Twenty of the most trusted technicians in the royal service were at various stations monitoring incoming data. On the large central monitor was drone footage of Atlantis.

The crystal city floated there with serene indifference. After Jemma and the spy plane unmasked them, whoever was running the place hadn't bothered to cloak the city again. It seemed almost a sign of the contempt in which they held their enemies. The crystal towers hadn't taken a shot at the drone either. Jemma wasn't sure what to make of it and what she didn't understand made her nervous.

"Have you spoken to the Alliance?" Jemma asked.

"Given their indifference during the last crisis," the king said, "I saw little point reaching out this time."

Jemma understood his bitterness, but this was hardly the time to hold a grudge. If the Alliance had any intel on their enemy, it would be foolish beyond words not to reach out.

"Do you think we should launch a preemptive strike?" the king asked.

"There are risks either way. An attack would be easy to justify given their earlier downing of our plane. A less-than-fatal blow might provoke them to retaliate. Since we have no idea what their weapons are capable of, caution might be the wiser course."

"My thoughts exactly," the king said. "The Ministry of War is less than pleased. I understand their position, but until we have more information, I'm not authorizing a strike."

"You have the Ministry of Magic's full support."

"Thank you for that." The king scrubbed a hand across his

weary face. Jemma doubted he'd gotten more than a few hours' sleep a night since Morgana's attack. "I suppose it couldn't hurt to contact the Alliance. This is potentially as big a threat to them as it is to us. You should do the same."

Jemma was taken aback, prompting the king to smile. "I'm well aware that you keep in touch with the boy wizard. And I approve. We owe him a great debt. Had he not defeated Morgana, god knows what the world would look like today."

She bowed. "As you wish, Majesty."

They parted ways and she went to call Dean Blane. Her ability to keep in touch with Conryu was limited by the fact that he spent so much time in places with no cell phone reception. He also apparently didn't trust her enough to give her one of those rune stones that let his friends contact him in the library.

Still, if anyone knew what was happening, it would be Dean Blane.

## CHAPTER 19

Conryu stepped out of the library and into a tropical jungle. All around him were tall trees, hanging vines, and red flowers the size of his head. The small clearing where he and Kai arrived was the first opening in the dense undergrowth he'd seen during his long survey of the island. The heat and humidity took his breath away. How could this island be so different from the one where he lived?

According to Maria, this island actually spent two months over the arctic. In that kind of cold, there shouldn't be any growth like this. He shook his head. Despite the power magic gave him, sometimes Conryu really hated it.

"How will we search the entire island, Chosen?" Kai asked.

"We won't. Even though the islands are a sealed environment, there are still minor spirits living here. Nothing with a real personality like a sprite or dryad, but still enough to let us know if anything strange has happened in the last few days."

He closed his eyes and focused. If there was any danger, he trusted Kai to deal with it. His thoughts and magic reached out to the wind spirits. If any of them were going to notice something, it would be the spirits of the wind.

There weren't many, but he finally found one with enough presence to respond to his call.

*Has anything happened here?*

It didn't seem to understand his question. That was the problem with dealing with the weakest spirits. They existed on the very edge of sentience.

*Have you seen anyone strange?*

He got a vague impression of his and Kai's faces.

Controlling his annoyance, he clarified. *Besides us.*

The spirit radiated joy when it finally understood what he wanted. An image appeared of another face, female and flawless, like she was wearing a glass mask. That was promising.

*Show me where.*

He opened his eyes and a faint blue spark appeared in front of him.

Kai reached for her sword, but he shook his head. "Our guide. The spirits have seen someone. Let's go."

They set out into the jungle. Conryu conjured a dark magic aura that disintegrated any vine or branch that might have delayed their travel. Even with that helping them, it took almost an hour to reach another clearing. As soon as they set foot in the little patch of grass, the blue spark vanished.

He sent his thanks to the spirit and focused on the matter at hand, a clear crystal obelisk three feet tall.

"What is it?" Kai asked.

"Beats me. Prime?"

"I don't know," the scholomantic growled between clamped teeth.

Conryu pointed and loosed a weak stream of fire. The spell hit the crystal, doing no damage, but not being negated either.

What exactly was the bloody thing doing? It had to be what caused the island to fall out of the sky, but now it was just sitting there, inert.

He stepped closer and reached out.

Kai grabbed his shoulder. "What are you doing?"

"Checking for a vibration. My guess is, whatever this thing is supposed to do, it must work like the testing crystal. Something has to trigger it. If there's no vibration, then it isn't active."

"I'll test it," Kai said. "You stay back."

Conryu didn't like putting others in danger, but Kai could be as stubborn as Maria at times. "Okay but be quick."

She nodded, darted in, and put her palm on the crystal.

Nothing happened.

After a few seconds she stepped back. "I felt nothing."

"Good. Let's put some distance between us and whatever that is and I'll see if I can smash it."

"Shouldn't we bring it to your mother?" Kai asked.

"I'm sure she'd like to check it out, but the only way to get it out of here is through the library and no way am I taking that crystal into the library. Who knows what kind of damage it might do?"

They backed up to the edge of the clearing and he brought the staff out from its pocket dimension. He leveled it at the crystal and the gem at the tip turned white. A lightning bolt lanced out, hit the crystal, and deflected into a tree, blowing ten feet of the trunk to splinters and sending it toppling to the ground.

Next the gem turned black and he hit the crystal with a blast of pure dark magic. All the grass around it withered and died, but the crystal itself didn't get a mark. Fire had already proven to be a loser and cold was equally worthless.

When he'd cycled through all the elements, Conryu frowned and scratched his chin. Destroying things usually wasn't a problem for him, but this crystal was proving especially durable. Then again maybe he was just approaching this from the wrong direction. The crystals seemed designed to defeat his magic. Something cruder might be the way to go.

The gem turned brown and Conryu pointed it at the ground near the far edge of the clearing. As his command, two boulders as big as his upper body ripped themselves free of the ground. He directed them to either side of the crystal and smashed them together.

A tinkling like shattering glass filled the air. He grinned and tossed the boulders aside. The obelisk had been reduced to hundreds of finger-length shards. "Bingo! Blunt physical force is the way to go. Let's check the other islands. The last thing we need is to have more of these things falling out of the sky."

Angus and Sienna left Conryu's building in Sentinel City disappointed. His mother hadn't been home and there was no indication of where she might have gone. A quick call to the Research Department got him the short reply that she was no longer employed there. That had surprised him more than not finding her at home. From what Angus understood, she loved that job. Something serious must have happened if she either quit or got fired.

When they reached the sidewalk Sienna asked, "Now what? You told me the mother could put me in touch with Conryu."

"Hey, it's not my fault she wasn't home. I'm not a psychic. The next best bet will be his girlfriend, but she's at the wizards' academy near Central. Can you magic us there?"

"No." Sienna grimaced. "I'm not powerful enough to open a proper portal. I can shift myself, but no one else."

"If you show up alone, you're going to get into trouble. Strange wizards aren't welcomed at the Academy. I guess we'll have to take the train. Do you have money for a ticket?"

She reached into her pocket and pulled out a gold coin. "Is this enough?"

Angus looked around but no one was paying attention to them. "That's plenty, though they don't take gold coins at the station. Tell you what. I'll cover the tickets and you can pay me back."

She offered a shallow bow. "I accept your offer. Thank you."

He flagged down a cab and they made the drive across the city to the train station. Everything seemed so normal. There was no indication that the world knew a legendary city had returned. He hadn't expected the government to make a big announcement, but he figured there'd be some sign, an increased security presence at least.

"Do you think anyone knows Atlantis has returned?" Angus asked. He flicked a glance at the driver to see if the woman had made any note of his comment. Her gaze was focused on the traffic not them. Besides, driving a cab in this city, she probably heard stranger things every day.

"It is possible no one here knows," Sienna said. "The wizards would have felt the city's return, but they probably had no idea what it meant. The Kingdom of the Isles knows, I told them, but whether they shared that information I couldn't say."

The cab pulled up to the train station and Angus paid their fare. Hundreds of people were streaming in and out of the huge complex, most on their cellphones or chatting with a companion. It was the busiest transport hub in the city with trains coming and going all day and all night to every corner of the Alliance.

"What now?" Sienna asked.

"Now we hope we can get seats on the next train to Central. It'll be a six-hour wait if it's full."

Angus led the way up a long flight of stairs to the terminal. Overhead, flat-screen televisions were covered with arrival and departure times. The next train to Central left in an hour and a half. He started toward the ticket counter, but Sienna broke off and went to one of the many smaller tvs playing the news. She walked like a zombie, seemingly totally unaware of the people she was bumping into.

Muttering a curse on wizards in general, he hurried after her. Sienna stopped ten feet away from the tv. Apparently, there had been an accident in Madagascar. He read the text under the attractive brunette that was delivering the news. He blinked and read it again.

One of the floating islands had fallen out of the sky and destroyed a large section of the island's interior. In all of recorded history, no floating island had ever crashed like that. If they were going to start falling randomly out of the sky, that was a huge problem.

"What a mess," Angus said.

Sienna looked up as though just realizing he was there. "They've struck the first blow."

Angus took a moment to process that. Keeping his voice pitched low he said, "You think Atlantis brought down the island? Do they have that kind of power?"

"I'm certain they did it. Madagascar is the ancient homeland of Lemuria. Though nothing remains, the attack is symbolic, a blow to their ancient enemies. And they certainly have the power. When it comes to negating magic, they are second to none."

Angus took her arm gently, his throat tight. "Come on. We need to get to the Academy. Even if Conryu is out of touch, they need to know what's happening."

He'd get tickets on the next train even if he had to buy them from another passenger. After what he just saw, it was clear there was no time to waste.

## CHAPTER 20

Conryu and Kai left the floating island and its ruined obelisk behind and an instant later emerged on a second island. This one featured an open plain surrounded by jagged mountains. It looked like someone dropped a section of the Midwest of North America in a huge stone bowl. It was warm, but dry instead of humid. He half expected to see a herd of bison go trundling by.

Interesting as the change of scenery was, they had a job to do. Conryu closed his eyes and reached out to the local wind spirits. They had nothing of interest to report. It looked like whoever was setting the crystals in place hadn't reached this island yet.

Kai put her hand on his shoulder. "Chosen, something is coming."

Conryu's eyes snapped open and he looked where she was pointing. Way above them, higher than the mountain peaks, something – he squinted to try and get a better look but found the sun too bright – flew toward them. It wasn't a bird, not moving in such a straight line.

"Can you make it out?"

"Not yet," Kai said. "What should we do?"

Conryu looked around. There wasn't a ton of places to hide. "We wait and see who it is and what they want. Maybe we can come to some sort of understanding and avoid a fight."

Prime snorted and Conryu had to admit he wasn't likely to get his wish. Still, if he could avoid a fight, he'd prefer to.

The object, it had a rectangular shape, but he couldn't make out anything else, passed through the impenetrable barrier surrounding the island like it wasn't even there. Whoever they were, they had powerful anti-magic abilities. He'd have to use indirect magic to fight them. Just to be ready, Conryu reached out with earth magic and grabbed a trio of boulders buried under the prairie. He could jerk them out and crush any threat in a second.

Kai reached for her sword, but Conryu said, "Not yet. We don't want to look aggressive. Let them make the first move. Besides, I've seen you draw your sword. It's hardly necessary for you to have it in your hands."

She didn't argue which he appreciated.

As it got closer, the object resolved into a boat made of crystal. Not that he was going to say that out loud, he'd sound like a madman.

"What is that?" Kai asked.

"Just what it looks like. I've never seen or heard of anything like it. Have you?"

Kai shook her head.

"Prime?"

The scholomantic's jaws were clamped so tightly together that his cover was bunching up. Flying crystal boats were apparently another thing he wasn't free to talk about.

The boat landed a hundred feet away from them. Seated inside was a single, distinctly female, figure made entirely of crystal. Golden energy swirled through its... her... Conryu wasn't sure how to classify the person. She stood, stepped out of the boat, and turned to face them. Her crystal face betrayed no emotion as she studied them.

"Hello," Conryu said. "I'm Conryu Koda and this is my friend, Kai. The surly looking book is Prime. This is going to sound strange, but you didn't happen to leave a crystal obelisk on another of the islands, did you?"

"Two children of Lemuria, and one a male. How remarkable." The crystal woman had a musical voice that sounded a bit like wind chimes. "This must be my lucky day."

Conryu had no idea what Lemuria was. He glanced at Kai who shrugged.

"Lemuria was the first kingdom of magic," Prime said. "They developed the first version of modern magic with the direct aid of the spirits."

"Finally, something you can talk about," Conryu said. He turned back to the crystal woman. "What should we call you?"

"Death!"

The crystal woman slammed her wrists together, filling the air with the most discordant, ear-rending noise.

Light flashed in Conryu's eyes as he struggled to remain conscious.

Kai rushed toward her, sword drawn.

The crackling black blade slammed into the woman's shoulder and shattered.

Kai rolled under a backhanded blow, sprang to her feet, and threw her ruined weapon aside.

The noise had died enough that he could think again. His first thought was to pull the boulders he'd tagged and hurl them toward their opponent.

The ground trembled as the stones ripped free and raced toward the crystal woman.

When they were only a few feet away, she punched them, smashing the rock as easily as Conryu might break a board in the dojo.

The crystal woman pointed.

Conryu leapt away just ahead of a red ray that burned a path through the grass behind him.

Enough playing around. "Reaper's Cloak! Dread Scythe!"

Two of his most powerful spells settled around him. Time to see how she handled this.

Conryu raced toward her, the transformed staff raised and ready to lop her crystal head off.

The crystal woman pointed again.

Wait until she saw her magic was useless against the cloak.

*Dodge!*

The Reaper's voice so surprised Conryu he almost ignored it. Years of training saved him. At the last second, he jumped right, evading the red ray. It barely caught the trailing end of the cloak, burning a chunk of it away.

Despite his surprise, Conryu continued his attack. The Dread Scythe came down hard on his opponent's raised arm. Instead of slicing it off, the enchanted weapon just bounced off.

"How?"

*My power is useless against Atlantean magic, as is all other elemental magic. Flee or die, boy.*

Great, how was he supposed to win without magic?

Conryu leapt another ray that would have taken his legs off at the knee.

He released his worthless spells and enhanced his body, making himself stronger and faster. Now he needed some kind of weapon.

"Chosen!" Kai was standing in the crystal woman's boat. "She has more of the obelisks in here."

"Stay away from those." The crystal woman thrust her palm at Kai and a shockwave blew her into the air.

With his enhanced speed, Conryu ran and caught her. "You okay?"

"Yes, thank you. There are three more obelisks."

He might not be able to defeat this enemy, but maybe he could at least eliminate the threat of the floating islands falling on more cities. "Can you keep her busy for a few seconds?"

"I can try."

Kai leapt at the crystal woman, kicked her in the face, sprang off, and spun away. She should be okay for a few seconds. He needed to focus.

Reaching deep into the earth, Conryu latched on to a stone bigger than his motorcycle. With a great heave of magic, he pulled it free. Dirt flew everywhere, blinding him for a moment.

A powerful force slammed into the stone, smashing it into chunks. Through the dust, he spotted the crystal woman pointing her raised palm at what was left of the rock.

"You will not ruin my work," the crystal woman said. "Your miserable kind have done enough harm to us."

Conryu was pretty sure he would have remembered offending people made of crystal. She must have been talking about wizards in general. Not that Conryu had heard anything about crystal people being at odds with wizards.

It didn't matter anyway. Even broken the mass of rock was enough to do what he needed.

He slapped his hands together and stone obliged his will by hammering into the crystal boat until nothing remained but shiny shards.

"Kai! Time to go."

The ninja appeared beside him, a nasty bruise on her cheek. "I was little help, Chosen. Apologies."

He opened the library door and they backed in followed by the crystal woman's roar of frustration.

🝊

Merik, Tanidel, and Curly flew through the bright, clear sky above their army of crystal soldiers while Larry marched along at the head of the column. Since their transformation, the force had destroyed three villages, killing dozens and taking scores more to add to their number. They hadn't faced more than a token resistance. Not surprising considering that anyone that might have resisted in anything resembling an organized way was already a crystal soldier.

He felt sick just thinking about it. When he agreed to free Atlantis, no mention was made of this butchery. He'd thought he was righting an old wrong, but now he wondered if the wizards of ancient times weren't right to try and wipe out the Atlanteans.

He kept that thought buried as deep as possible lest Tanidel pick it up. She still treated him kindly, but his lack of enthusiasm for the mission had made her distant. And to think he'd once deceived himself into believing she might be his future wife.

The stupidity of that notion was now obvious. What was less obvious was what he was going to do about it. Or even if he was going to do anything. With his feeble abilities he wouldn't last five seconds in a fight with his so-called allies.

A fourth town, the biggest one so far, appeared on the horizon. The spire of a church jutted up, marking the center of the town. Even with his enhanced vision, Merik saw no people out and about. Maybe they had spotted the army approaching and were hiding. He hoped they'd run far and fast away from here. Not that hiding did much good.

Somehow the Atlanteans sniffed them out no matter where they went.

"We're going to scout ahead," Tanidel said, he assumed for his benefit. Larry and Curly hadn't spoken to him since they left the archbishop's palace.

The crystal boat zipped forward. They made a full circle around the town and it turned out to be as empty as he'd hoped. No one would die or be changed, not today anyway.

They landed in the town square, a small park with a fountain in the center, and got out. "They must have gotten wind of our approach," Merik said.

Curly shot him a withering glare. It was an obvious thing to say, but the constant silence wore on him. It wasn't natural, at least for living people. Living statues, on the other hand, seemed to revel in it.

*We've hit a setback.* The voice of one of the Atlanteans that remained behind jabbed into his brain with all the subtlety of an ice pick. *After our initial success in bringing down one of the islands, our remaining negation crystals were destroyed in battle.*

*With who?* Curly demanded.

*A male wizard and his ally. His power was considerable and though no direct threat to us, it was enough to destroy the crystals and one of our flyers. The city has also been discovered.*

A ripple of surprise and concern passed through the link.

*Already?* That was Tanidel's psychic voice. *We assumed it would take months for the wizards to locate it.*

*We assumed wrong. The technology available now is greater than we realized. They have made no move against us yet, but it is only a matter of time. As such, we must act quickly against the wizards, put them on the defensive. How many soldiers have you gathered?*

*Eight hundred and seventy.* That was Larry. He seemed to be primarily in charge of controlling the crystal soldiers.

*That will have to be enough to begin. I have dispatched*

*transport ships to collect you. Merik and Tanidel, you will need to collect our sister stranded on the floating island. We have two primary targets, the largest collections of wizards in the world.*

As suddenly as it appeared, the voice vanished. Tanidel and Merik got back in the boat and took to the air. No further words were exchanged. Or if they were, Merik wasn't included in the conversation.

When they were high in the sky he asked, "What will we do after we rescue our marooned sister?"

"Return to Atlantis. There are two targets, one for each of the others. They are more than capable of controlling that many crystal soldiers on their own. Our duty is to keep the city safe. Should the wizards be stupid enough to attack, they will learn just how powerful we have become."

She sounded confident, but through their connection he could feel her doubts. The early discovery of the city had thrown her. Merik found himself in the strange position of not knowing who to root for.

The flight didn't take terribly long and before he knew it, they were landing in the middle of a field that looked like a herd of mad elephants had dug it up. Standing as still as the statue she resembled was the stranded Atlantean. The remains of her boat lay scattered across the torn earth a few paces from where she stood.

"What happened?" Tanidel asked as she stepped aboard.

"I found a male wizard and his companion here when I arrived to place the crystal. We fought. While they were no match for me, the male did manage to destroy the crystals and my transport."

"Conryu Koda," Merik muttered. "To think you'd run into him of all people."

Tanidel and Moe – Merik figured he might as well keep

with his naming convention – stared at him as they rose up and off the island.

"What? There's only one male wizard. Everyone knows who he is. Apparently, he's the most powerful wizard in the world and on the outs with the Alliance government."

"If he is the strongest wizard this world can muster," Moe said. "Then we have little to fear."

Merik figured that was kind of arrogant given that Moe was the one left stranded, not Conryu, but he kept his opinion to himself.

No matter who was right, it seemed the battle was going to begin in earnest.

## CHAPTER 21

Conryu and Kai checked the remaining islands and destroyed one more obelisk. No more of the crystal people showed up and he allowed himself to hope that they had dealt with all the magic-negating crystals. Having one less danger to worry about was a pleasant feeling, though, he expected, a temporary one.

They returned to the library to travel back to the Academy. The others weren't going to believe what had happened. Living crystal statues, that had to be a first.

"Chosen, I require a new weapon," Kai said.

"Yeah, where does one go to buy new magical ninja swords?"

"I can get one from the armory at our village. The black swords are strong, but hardly unbreakable."

"You don't think the others would have brought them to the monastery?" he asked.

"The grandmaster said she intends to maintain a small presence in our ancestral home for as long as possible. Spare weapons will have been left behind for those on guard duty."

Kai looked away, staring at the library floor. "I don't wish to tell Kanna of my failure, not until I have redeemed myself by taking that crystal woman's head."

Conryu put a hand on her shoulder. "You have nothing to be embarrassed about. My magic wasn't much more use than your sword. She can't complain about you losing to an enemy powerful enough to beat my death incarnate spell. Come on, let's get you a sword. Without that hilt over your shoulder you look half dressed."

She offered him a pity smile for his lame joke and Conryu willed the library to shift to Ninja Island as he'd named it. The doors opened in the middle of the village rather than at the circle where they first arrived. Nothing had changed in the last few days which argued his barrier was holding and the Iron Emperor hadn't settled on a way to bypass it. Maybe he didn't have any flying constructs.

A trio of ninjas appeared and took a knee in front of him. "How may we serve, Chosen?"

"Kai needs a new sword. All quiet here?"

"One wave of stone soldiers appeared but were felled by your spell. Other than that, all is well."

"Great. Do what you have to, Kai. Prime and I will check the wards on the Hell gate just to make sure everything's secure."

Kai hesitated and one of the other ninjas said, "We will watch over him while you rearm, sister."

She bowed and ran off to one of the smaller huts. Conryu hardly needed protection out here, but if it made her feel better, he wouldn't complain. He found the path into the jungle and set out. The Hell gate threw off so much dark energy he could sense it easily.

"From a distance all seems as it should be," Prime said.

"Given the power of your wards, they are hardly likely to deteriorate this quickly."

"I know. Kai seemed like she needed some time to gather herself. If I'm not around, maybe she'll relax a little."

Five minutes later they reached the clearing. The black disk of the Hell gate looked exactly as he left it. Nothing was coming out of it that wasn't supposed to, and the tendrils running to his barrier were solid and unwavering.

"Told you," Prime said.

*You survived a brush with the Atlantean. I'm impressed.*

The Reaper's voice surprised him less than the information it conveyed. "Atlantean? That crystal woman was from Atlantis?"

*Indeed. The spirits' agent has failed to prevent their return. Now the war will resume.*

"We need to have a serious, face-to-face talk. Can we meet somewhere in Hell?"

*Come to my palace in the Black City. Either of your bonded demons can guide you. The injunction has outlived its usefulness. If your world is to survive, you must be told everything. Do not delay.*

"I'll be there as fast as I can. But I need a favor."

"Master, this isn't—" Prime's words were cut off by the Reaper.

*You dare ask me for a favor? I am not your friend or your servant. I am a god.*

"Come on, it's just a little thing. Kai was really close with the former grandmaster. From what I understand, she's supposed to be serving you as a dark angel. I just wanted to arrange a few minutes for them to talk, give her a chance to say goodbye. That's no problem for you, is it?"

*Why I ever chose such a soft-hearted fool is beyond me. You're lucky you're powerful, boy, or I might cut you loose and find another.*

"So you'll arrange it?"

*Yes, now hurry.*

The Reaper's presence vanished and Conryu grinned. He was finally going to get some answers.

"You're lucky he didn't kill you on the spot," Prime said. "Bargaining with the Reaper isn't healthy."

"I suspect he needs me. He said it himself, there's no reason for me to be his chosen. Our personalities are too different. Come on, let's find Kai and go. The longer we make him wait, the crabbier he'll get. What's the Black City like?"

"It's a huge city at the center of Hell. There are demons everywhere, souls are traded the way you humans trade stocks, and there are no laws beyond the strong can do what they want. It's basically the most dangerous place in existence."

"So you're saying we shouldn't look for a vacation home?"

Prime snorted, drawing another grin. The most dangerous city in existence, what could go wrong?

---

Jemma was with the king in the secure ops center when Atlantis's crystal ship crossed into Kingdom airspace. A second drone had been dispatched to shadow the vessel. It was shaped like a flat-bottomed landing craft, fully sealed. The only thing visible was the shiny outer walls. What was inside remained a mystery. Somehow, she doubted it would be anything good.

"Do we have any way to communicate with them?" the king asked the room at large.

"They've remained silent despite hailing them on all radio frequencies," the lead comms officer said.

He looked to Jemma who shook her head. "We've tried magic of all sorts. Our spells just bounce off the hull. Much as I dislike agreeing with the Ministry of War, I fear force is our only option to stop them."

The king looked hopefully around the room, but all stations remained silent. He sagged and said, "So be it. Have the RAF scramble fighters. That drone is armed, correct?"

"Yes, Majesty," the pilot said.

"Fire at will."

The image on the main screen turned and the crosshairs changed from green to red. A missile shot out, a trail of white smoke hiding its path. A second later it slammed into the side of the crystal ship. Silent flames erupted and died almost as quickly.

When the drone completed its turn, they got their first clear view of the impact site. The side of the enemy ship didn't have a mark on it.

Stunned silence filled the room. That missile carried a five-hundred-pound warhead. It should have at least chipped the hull.

"Hit it again," the king ordered.

The image shifted as the drone came around for another shot. Three-quarters of the way through, a protrusion grew out of the hull. It glowed red and shot out a lance of energy.

The screen went blank.

"Drone down, Majesty," the pilot said.

The king looked at Jemma, eyes pleading. "Tell me there's something we can do to stop them."

Jemma wished she could, but everything they'd seen indicated that magic was useless against the Atlanteans. If conventional weapons were equally ineffective, she was out of ideas.

The main monitor came back to life. The enemy ship continued to make its way through the sky at a steady pace.

"New drone on station, Majesty," the pilot said. "Shall I make another attack run?"

"No, just observe for now," the king said. "Status of our fighters?"

"On the way," the RAF liaison said. "Contact in under a minute."

"Tell them to try bullets instead of missiles," Jemma said.

"Why bullets?" the king asked.

"We already know missiles don't work, so why not? Besides, I want to see something. Bullets will answer my question better than missiles."

The liaison was looking at the king. He said, "Do it."

Orders were relayed and they all waited for the jets to come roaring in. They didn't have to wait long. The first Firehawk came in at high speed and raked the ship with 12mm rounds before banking away to avoid an energy blast.

No damage was done, but now Jemma understood why. The bullets were stopped short of impact by an invisible energy field. It must have stopped the missiles the same way. It was an impenetrable barrier much like the ones surrounding the floating islands.

"I need to make a phone call," Jemma said. "Excuse me, Majesty."

Not waiting for permission, she hurried out of the command center and down a hall to where her phone could get a signal. Dean Blane's number was in her contact list and she dialed it.

"Are you tracking the crystal ship?" Jemma asked.

"Yes, it's halfway across the Atlantic and coming fast. The Air Force is getting ready to intercept before it reaches land."

"Tell them not to waste their time. Those ships are protected by a barrier. It turns aside bullets and missiles. We have one over our territory now and it's turned aside everything we've thrown at it. I was hoping you might have an idea what we might try."

"Just a sec." The silence dragged on for what felt like hours but couldn't have been more than a minute. "Jemma, Mrs. Kane suggests you try hitting it with something slow and heavy."

"Why? And what's Conryu's mother doing there?"

"She's consulting. She says it's something to do with velocity and vibrations. It's science stuff and I don't really get it. It's also all we've got right now. If you do try, let us know how it goes."

"Okay, thanks." Jemma hung up.

What was she supposed to do? The RAF didn't have low-speed weapons. Maybe the experts would have an idea.

She hurried back to the command center and told them what Dean Blane said. "Anyone know what we could hit them with that's slow and heavy?"

"How about the drone?" the pilot said.

"Explain," the king demanded.

"I could fly it straight up and kill the engine. It weighs about half a ton. If that's not heavy enough I don't know what would be."

Before the king could give an order one way or the other, the radar operator said, "Enemy craft is slowing and starting to descend."

"Location?" the king asked.

A map of the island appeared on one of the side monitors. It zoomed in and Jemma's heart lurched. The ship was almost directly over the Kingdom's wizard school.

Jemma needed to evacuate the students. "I have to go."

"Do what you must," the king said. "And God go with you."

## CHAPTER 22

Cerberus raced through the darkness of Hell with Kai and Conryu on his back. The invitation, or perhaps summons would be a better word, to attend the Reaper at his palace had left Kai speechless. Conryu supposed it wasn't every day you got to meet your god, especially when you were still alive.

"Is there any protocol I should know about?" Conryu asked.

"I don't know, Chosen. A living Daughter of the Reaper being called to the palace has never happened, at least not as far as I know."

"Besides," Prime added. "You wouldn't follow it even if there was."

"I might, if it wasn't too ridiculous."

Cerberus barked, drawing his attention away from his companions. A light appeared in the darkness ahead, or maybe it was many lights fused into one. He couldn't fully grasp the size of the city from this distance, but it appeared to cover much of the horizon. That would make it even bigger than Tokyo.

"The Black City has no defined size beyond what the Reaper wishes it to be," Prime said. "If he so desired, it could cover the entirety of Hell, right up to the border of the mortal realm."

"Wow." Conryu knew the Reaper was powerful but being able to change the size of a city at will was amazing.

"Powerful isn't the right word, Master," Prime said. "In Hell, he's omnipotent. The Reaper's will controls everything."

Conryu swallowed. Maybe he should have been more polite.

Too late now. The edge of the city was only moments away.

There was no subtle transition from darkness to city, it was basically nothing then a road lined with three-story stone buildings that wouldn't have looked out of place in a medieval town. The stone was dark and grungy and cloth canopies dangled limp in the still air.

On the roof of one of the buildings, a bat-winged demon leered down at them, its red eyes gleaming. A bark from Cerberus sent it fleeing deeper into the city.

He and Kai climbed down. Cerberus gave a worried whimper.

"Don't worry, we'll be fine." Conryu patted his flank. "Hopefully this won't take long."

They hadn't even started down the nearest street when a familiar presence approached. The Dark Lady appeared in front of him looking lovely as always.

"Master, why are you here? It isn't safe."

"The head man himself called for me."

"The Reaper summoned you?" The fear in her voice made him nervous for a moment but he shook it off. He needed to know what only the demon lord could tell him.

"Yeah, how about you show us the way?"

"I can do better than that." She held out her pale hands.

Conryu took one and after a moment's hesitation Kai took the other. An instant later they stood facing the imposing gate of a massive fortress. A black wall hundreds of feet high was studded with impaled heads. Beyond the wall, a madman's idea of a castle loomed. Dozens of turrets and towers sprouted from the main keep. Black pennants snapped in a breeze he couldn't feel. In the skies, black-winged figures soared in lazy circles.

"Are those the black angels?" Conryu asked.

"Yes." Kai's voice was thin with awe. "Hundreds of generations of my sisters patrol these skies."

A deep, dull clank sounded and the gate began to open. Beyond the gap stood a pair of black angels. They were dressed in black like Kai, including a mask. A pair of swords rode on their backs between seven-foot-wide raven wings. They made beautiful guards if nothing else.

"Do you wish me to join you, Master?" the Dark Lady asked, her voice trembling.

"You can wait here."

Conryu and Kai walked through the gates and towards the guards. He assumed they were for show. After all, what use did an omnipotent demon lord have for guards?

The right-hand black angel said, "The master is expecting you. Follow me."

They fell in behind her and the fortress shifted around them. In three steps they were standing in front of another door, this one ten foot tall, black, and carved with Infernal runes. At his approach the runes glowed and the door swung open.

Conryu stepped into the darkness beyond. When Kai tried to follow, the black angel said, "You will wait here. The master desires to speak with his chosen alone."

Kai bowed. It was the first time he'd gone anywhere on his

own without her offering a word of complaint. But after all it wasn't like she could protect him from the Reaper.

The door slammed shut behind him and crimson lights burst into being. At the end of a blood-red carpet was a throne made from skulls, all of them different. Beside it was a glass cylinder as tall as Conryu and filled with a multitude of yellow lights.

A giant cloaked in black sat on the throne, a gleaming black scythe at his side. The Reaper radiated power unlike anything Conryu had ever sensed. He made Lucifer feel like a child, an insect even. It took all Conryu's strength of will to stay standing and not fall into a little ball and weep.

"Welcome to the center of Hell," the Reaper said. "You are the first of my chosen to be so honored in ages."

"Thanks. Tell me about Atlantis and the crystal people."

"Long ago, the people of Atlantis were magical researchers, brilliant, innovative, focusing on crystal magic. It's rare on this world, less so on others. The other spirit lords and I gave our blessing to a different people, the Lemurians. They were the progenitors of modern wizards. Two diverging paths that in time would have come together as a greater whole. But that all changed when one of the city's most gifted researchers discovered a new source of power, a forbidden source."

"What sort of power would be forbidden?" Conryu asked.

"There's only one, the power of the void, of oblivion. To tap the power is to risk ending all of existence. We couldn't let them continue to exploit such a dangerous power source. The spirit lords agreed that we had no choice but to wipe them out before they could fully master their new energy. The war was long and brutal and, in the end, only my followers had the will to take the measures necessary for victory. A death curse was placed on Atlantis, one that would have killed them all in weeks. Somehow they escaped and some survived."

"Like the crystal woman I fought. I've battled demons less powerful than her."

"Their crystal bodies are connected to the void. It grants them great power and protection from magic. The only way to defeat them is to crack their shell and destroy the soul within."

"Is that all?" Conryu shook his head. "I hit her with a boulder and she smashed it to pieces without chipping a nail. How am I supposed to crack her shell?"

The Reaper stood. "The Atlanteans aren't the only ones that have been preparing for this battle. Come, I will show you Hell's arsenal."

Kai paced outside the throne room door. It was hard to believe she was really here. Awe and concern warred within her. She shouldn't worry. Deep inside she knew even if she'd gone with Conryu, she would have been helpless if the Reaper had decided to slay him. In fact, if the order had come, she would have been bound to kill him herself.

Or try to. Kai held no illusions about the difference between her and Conryu's power. And if it came right down to it, she might risk an eternity of suffering to avoid hurting him. It was disloyal to even think that, especially here, but she refused to lie to herself. Her first loyalty was to Conryu. Come what may, their fate was now linked.

"You always did think too much."

That voice. She'd believed she'd never hear it again, not before she died at least.

Kai spun and found a black angel walking toward her. She was dressed exactly the same as all the others, but there was something in her stride that Kai recognized.

"Grandmaster Narumi."

Narumi undid her mask, revealing a younger, but still familiar face. In fact, she looked much like Kanna. Only strict training kept Kai from breaking into tears.

"This generation's chosen is an odd one," Narumi said. "He demanded that we have a chance to meet before agreeing to come see the master. What's odder is that the Reaper agreed. It is good to see you, Kai."

Kai's mind spun. Conryu had done this for her? She could hardly believe it. When they left, she would have to thank him properly.

"And you, Grandmaster. When we arrived on the island and Kanna said you had fallen in battle I was shocked."

"No reason to be," Narumi said. "I was getting old. A single step too slow is all it takes. Better I fell in battle than became a burden."

"You wouldn't have been a burden. Your wisdom would have been a boon to the Daughters."

Narumi laughed. "You were always a sweet child. Your work with the chosen has been exemplary. I didn't get a chance to tell you in life, but I was proud of what you accomplished. A greater threat now looms. Walk with me."

Kai glanced back at the door and chewed her lip.

"He's not in there anymore. The master has taken him to our armory. The Reaper has been agitated lately and he rarely gets agitated. He says nothing to us, but something's happening on your world that has him worried. And anything that worries the Reaper had best worry everyone else."

As they walked together down the gloomy halls Kai said, "You said my world. Are there others where the Reaper has interests?"

"Do you know the greatest thing about being a dark angel? It's having the veil of ignorance lifted from your eyes. There is so much that we can't understand as short-sighted mortals.

Our awareness is too limited. Focus on your duties and the challenges you face. The rest will be waiting when your time arrives."

"So you're not going to answer my question?" Kai asked.

"Not today. For now, all I'll say is that the universe is a big place, far bigger than you can imagine." A door appeared ahead of them as though out of nowhere. "Here we are."

Narumi opened the door and noise, pounding, grinding, ear-bleeding noise, washed over Kai. She had never encountered such a cacophony before. Dozens of anvils were occupied by demonic smiths hammering weapons out of black metal. She wanted to ask if this was where their swords came from but doubted the grandmaster would hear her question over the noise.

They made their way through the forge and to another door on the opposite side. Beyond it was another massive room, blessedly silent. Racks upon racks of weapons filled it to bursting. Swords, maces, axes, anything Kai could imagine and many things she'd never dreamed of and doubted were made to fit a human's hand.

"Why!" Kai winced at her shout. "Why aren't there any modern weapons?"

"Weapons based on technology tend to be useless against magical foes. Hell's enemies need to be faced blade to blade. Come, your chosen is waiting."

Conryu hefted a spike-backed mace made of black metal. It was about two feet long and the head was round with a single, six-inch, pyramidal spike jutting out of it. The whole thing crackled with dark magic. There were a hundred of them in crates on the ground in front of him.

The Reaper had brought him out to this courtyard where the weapons were waiting. He said nothing as Conryu examined them. They certainly looked like they'd penetrate heavy crystal. In fact, Conryu couldn't remember seeing such a brutal weapon. Of course, there was one obvious problem.

"Any non-dark aligned person touching one of these things is liable to get their hands melted off."

"Naturally," the Reaper said. "Anyone capable of using one of my weapons is apt to be loyal to me. It's an anti-theft precaution. They were made to be used by the Daughters. I formed the group specifically to battle the Atlanteans should they ever return."

That made sense. Having a skilled and dedicated force just waiting to fight your greatest enemy was smart. Unfortunately, it meant sending people he had come to think of as friends if not family into danger. There was no way around it, but he didn't have to like it.

"So how do they work?" Conryu asked.

"Simple. The spike is driven through the magic-blocking outer shell where it releases a burst of dark magic that destroys the enemy's soul. Repeat until all Atlanteans are dead."

Brutal for sure. "Okay, assuming we can defeat them all, how do I deal with this void power you're so worried about? I assume it's not something I can just dispel."

"No. If it was that simple, the Lemurians would have won the war easily. To defeat the threat of Atlantis you must accomplish three things. One, kill all the true people of Atlantis. You will know them because they are far more powerful than any of the other foes you might face."

"Like the crystal woman?"

"Exactly. There are twelve of them. Next you have to destroy the Heart of Atlantis, a massive crystal that directs the void magic and powers their crystal weapons. Finally, you must find the void pit and seal it, repairing the damage to reality."

Conryu put the mace he was holding back in the open case at his feet. "Okay, the first two are straightforward enough, but how do I go about repairing a hole in reality?"

"All of reality is composed of the four elements and bound together by the Creator's light. You will have to weave those five elements together around the opening, creating a scab of sorts. In a few thousand years the damage will fully heal."

"No offense, but I haven't the slightest idea how to even begin such a spell."

"Of course you don't." The Reaper turned his faceless cowl on Conryu. "No mortal mind is capable of such a casting. As the chosen of all elements, you must open your mind to the spirit lords and let them act through your body. You will be a vessel for their power."

"Is this why I was chosen by all of you?" Conryu asked. "Did you know Atlantis was about to return?"

"No. All we knew was that you were born with massive magical potential and should you decide to serve one element over another, it would give that spirit lord a huge advantage over the rest of us. It was decided that we would share you and thus avoid a potential conflict. That Atlantis happened to return now was simply a lucky break."

The fact that the spirits didn't know everything that lay in his future was oddly comforting. It implied that at least some of his future was his own to choose. On the other hand, it would have been nice to know he was going to live through the coming battle.

"Your bodyguard is returning. Take the weapons, win the war, and I will consider my investment in you well paid back."

"One more thing," Conryu dared ask.

Whatever the omnipotent demon lord equivalent to a sigh was escaped from the cowl. "What?"

"When I die, where do I end up? I mean, if every spirit lord has a claim on me, is my soul going to be torn into six pieces?"

"You will have the rarest of all opportunities. When your soul is finally freed from your body you will become a wandering soul, free to travel between all six realms. There are less than a dozen of them in all of reality. Consider yourself blessed. When you're ready, open a Hell gate here. It will exit in the Daughters' new home."

With that the Reaper vanished. He'd imparted a great deal of knowledge to Conryu and at the same time left him with almost as many new questions.

"Chosen!" He turned to see Kai running toward him.

She looked happier than he'd seen her since learning of the death of her mentor. The Reaper must have kept his promise.

"Ready to go? We have the weapons we need to fight back."

Kai lifted one of the maces. "I bet this will make that crystal bitch regret letting us escape."

Conryu grinned and opened a Hell gate. It was time to win a war.

# CHAPTER 23

When Jemma arrived at the school, things were calm and normal. The beautiful, manicured grounds were empty as students were busy in various classes. It was a beautiful day, not the sort of day you expected to get attacked by a legendary enemy most considered a myth.

She hurried across the yard to the administration building. Judging by the crystal ship's last position, she had about fifteen minutes to get everyone organized and safely out. There was no way that could happen, but she had to try.

As soon as she stepped into the administrative area the four secretaries on duty leapt to their feet. "Is everything okay, ma'am?" one of them asked.

"No. Assemble everyone in the auditorium. Tell the teachers and older students to begin evacuations according to plan omega. The enemy will be here in under a quarter of an hour. Is Sandy in her office?"

"Yes, ma'am," the secretary's voice held a quaver and all the blood had drained from her face. Jemma didn't like scaring people, but it was good that she was taking this seriously.

Leaving the four of them to get things organized, Jemma went down a long hall to the assistant dean's office. Technically her position as Ministry head also made her dean of the school, but she had so many duties outside of the grounds, Sandy handled the day-to-day things.

Jemma didn't bother knocking. She pushed the door open and found Sandy reading at her desk, her feet up and chair back. The younger woman scrambled to her feet. "Jemma, what is it?"

"Trouble. I've got the secretaries organizing an evacuation, but I need whoever you can muster to fight. We'll need to hold off the enemy for as long as we can."

Sandy frowned. "Who's attacking and where's the army?"

"Atlantis is attacking and the RAF has been trying to bring the ship down since it arrived in the skies. As for the army, that's not a bad idea. I'll arrange for them to be ready. You're wind aligned so you'll have to bring them here."

Jemma took out her phone and dialed the War Minister. "Thomas, I need whatever forces you can spare at the school and I need them now. Don't give me that bullshit. Do I really have to get his majesty to give the order? You know what's headed our way. I need time to get my students out. Okay, Sandy will be there to pick them up in ninety seconds."

"We good?" Sandy asked.

"Yes. They're expecting you at Fort Keene. Bring as many as are ready the moment you arrive. Drop them in the central courtyard. I'll be waiting."

Sandy nodded and vanished into a wind portal.

Jemma left the office and made her way to the auditorium. Students rushed past her through the halls, guided by their teachers. They looked nervous, but not panicked, not yet anyway. The teachers kept their voices calm, but the looks they threw Jemma's way told her all she needed to know.

They were right to be worried. At the front of the auditorium the senior light magic instructor was directing people to their seats. She spotted Jemma and met her at the base of the seats.

"You can't wait for everyone to gather," Jemma said before she could ask any questions. "Open portals and get them out as fast as you can."

"Is it that bad?"

"I don't know yet, but this enemy specializes in negating magic. The longer we wait, the better the odds that some of you will get stuck here. We need to get as many kids as possible to the secondary locations. But don't linger. Disperse them across the Kingdom until they're recalled. The more spread out the students are, the harder it will be for anyone to hunt them down."

Jemma gave the woman's shoulder an encouraging squeeze before hurrying out to the courtyard. The first soldiers would be arriving soon.

Luckily, she arrived just as the first wind portal opened. Soldier after soldier marched out. They wore body armor, helmets, and camouflage uniforms. Each carried a rifle over his shoulder and she was relieved to see a few had rocket launchers. The rifles, she suspected, would be of little use save as clubs, but maybe the explosives would do some damage.

Jemma smiled at her optimism. Nothing they'd seen so far indicated conventional weapons were worth a damn against the weapons of Atlantis.

A young man with shiny new lieutenant's bars on his collar hurried her way and saluted. "First infantry reporting for duty, ma'am. Where do you want us?"

"I want a defensive perimeter set up around the main building. You'll have to hold the enemy off long enough for the students to escape. This is going to be a hard fight; I won't sugarcoat it for you. The forces arrayed against us may be the most dangerous the Kingdom has ever fought and our magic is mostly useless against them. What I can do is raise an earthen barrier to hopefully slow them down."

Jemma's phone rang in the middle of her explanation. She listened, nodded to herself, and disconnected.

"The enemy vehicle is ten miles out. Contact in two minutes. Get your men in position while I raise the barrier."

He saluted and rushed back to his men, shouting orders and waving them toward the main building. Hopefully he would survive what was coming, but she didn't hold out much hope for any of them. Shaking her head Jemma touched the ground and chanted. She was far from an expert in earth magic, but she could raise a rampart easily enough. A four-foot-high barrier should slow whatever the Atlanteans threw at them and would let the soldiers shoot over it.

She joined them behind the barrier and looked up. In the distance, the crystal ship was visible maybe two miles out. It appeared undamaged. Whatever desperate attack the RAF made must not have amounted to much.

The ship approached slowly, as if eager to increase their fear. The soldiers clutched their rifles and watched the unnatural vessel come to a stop about a hundred yards away. On the bottom of its hull, four protrusions formed.

Jemma had seen those before. "Everyone down!"

She threw herself flat against the earthen barrier and sent magic into it, making the earth as hard as stone.

A moment later the first blast struck home.

More followed, pounding the rampart like a smith's

hammer on a stubborn piece of steel. Her magic held it together, repairing damage as fast as it appeared.

The barrage shifted to the school itself. If they thought it was an easy target, they'd badly underestimated the precautions Jemma's predecessors had taken.

The beams streaked in and bounced off an invisible energy field. The Atlanteans kept it up for a few seconds before giving up.

A high, clear chime rang out and all Jemma's magical protections fizzled out. The enemy had activated an anti-magic field. But how far did it extend?

"Lieutenant, put a round into the eaves of the school."

He stared at her for a moment, shrugged, and had one of his men fire. The bullet drove into the wood.

As she feared, the defensive barrier was down.

And if that was down, the escape portals wouldn't be working either.

"Ma'am, we've got incoming," one of the soldiers peeking over the bank said.

Jemma scrambled up and looked for herself. Dozens of crystal soldiers were leaping from an opening in the ship. They hit the ground with enough force to sink in to their ankles, but it did them no harm. As soon as they landed, they pulled themselves free and marched toward the earthworks.

"I need to check on the evacuation," Jemma said. "Can you hold them?"

"We'll do our best," the lieutenant said.

She couldn't ask for more than that.

Jemma ran toward the school. Escaping on foot was going to be a bigger challenge, but somehow she'd get those kids to safety.

In the few days since her secret eavesdropping on the president and his advisors, Malice had learned much more about his secret anti-magic project. Her sources indicated that it was a total failure. Assassins equipped with the crystals had been sent to eliminate Conryu Koda. He'd dealt with the fools easily, killing one and returning the rest unconscious and without their crystals.

She nearly laughed out loud when she heard. Much as she personally disliked the boy, he had been badly underestimated. That was a mistake Malice would never make. Somehow the scientists had also lost their remaining test subject leaving them with no crystals and nothing to show for their time and effort. They were beaten and she hadn't had to lift a finger. She savored such victories the most.

Now she had been summoned by the president to an emergency meeting. Apparently, some new threat had popped up, something bad enough that he was willing to set aside his dislike in the hope that she could help. He'd better believe that she'd remember this and make him pay for it later.

Today's meeting wasn't in the president's private office. Instead everyone was gathered in the situation room. It was three levels down in the basement. Malice had been forced to use pain-negating magic to make the long walk and even then, only managed it thanks to the elevator. The guards on duty outside, another pair of young men barely old enough to shave, opened the doors as she approached.

Even before she stepped through, the sounds of raised, panic-tinged voices reached her. Whatever was going on, it was serious. On a four-foot-wide screen mounted on the wall was a scene of chaos. Crystal humanoids were firing crimson rays at fleeing young people. Wizards were counterattacking, but their spells fizzled before striking home. Soldiers fired rifles to equally little effect.

The president's focus was on a smaller screen where a crystal ship flew through a clear sky. Malice ignored the many eyes on her and made her way to stand beside him.

"What's going on?" she asked.

"The wizard school in the Kingdom of the Isles is under attack by an unknown enemy." He pointed at the screen. "They arrived in a vessel exactly like this one. The RAF damaged it by crashing a drone into the top deck, but it repaired itself in seconds and kept on coming."

"And this one?" Malice asked.

"Ten minutes from the East Coast."

"Headed for the Academy?"

"That's our assumption, but all it is, is an assumption. If you know anything, have some secret weapon your researchers have been cooking up, now's the time to bring it out. Nothing we've tried has worked and we lost six jets trying."

"You mean something like a crystal that can negate magic?" Malice smiled her most evil smile when he looked down at her. "Yes, I know all about your desire not to have to rely on wizards anymore. Funny how when there's a real emergency, I'm the one you send for."

The muscle in his jaw bunched and relaxed. "That's a discussion for another time. Can you stop them?"

"I doubt it. Magic appears useless against them. I suggest you evacuate the school and try hitting them with something heavier than whatever your jets were carrying. I wouldn't hold your breath on it working."

His gaze was searching but Malice gave him nothing. The truth was, she really had no idea how to stop something immune to magic. This was exactly what she feared would happen if the president and his friends got their way. Now the nightmare had come to life and she was every bit as helpless as she'd feared. It was no consolation that the threat came from an unknown enemy rather than the man beside her.

## CHAPTER 24

Maria ran through the Academy toward the science lab where she'd left Conryu's mother working on her latest device. Speaking of Conryu, she'd been trying to reach him for an hour, but the rune stone failed to connect. She couldn't imagine where he was, but she really needed to talk to him. Dean Blane had gotten the evacuation order five minutes ago. An Atlantean ship was on its way. Apparently, they had already attacked the magic school in the Kingdom of the Isles to tragic effect.

She reached the door and pushed it open. Mrs. Koda was sitting exactly where Maria had left her, hunched over an oblong device, a soldering iron in her hand and magnifying lenses over her eyes.

"We have to go," Maria said.

Mrs. Koda looked up. "I'm almost done. I really think this sonic bomb is the key to beating them."

"In an hour a ship full of them is going to arrive. Dean Blane has ordered everyone out of here and on the train. You can work on it there. Please. Conryu would never forgive me if something happened to you."

Her smile was bittersweet. "Okay. Let me get a box to collect my things and we'll go."

Relieved, Maria murmured a quick spell and made a circle with her finger. A light magic bubble formed around her workbench. "Do you need anything else?"

"I believe that will do it."

They hurried out. Maria took them down one of the deserted back corridors in hopes of avoiding panicked students. It was odd that she wasn't losing it herself. Maybe she'd become used to this sort of thing considering all the trouble they'd gotten into over the past few years.

"Have you heard from Conryu?" Mrs. Koda asked.

Maria debated how much to tell her, but only for a moment. This wasn't the time to keep secrets. "Not for a while. Luckily Conryu isn't the sort of person you need to worry about."

"Easier said than done."

Maria sighed. Wasn't that the truth.

They reached the exit and stepped outside. Voices from the Academy's loading area indicated preparations were coming along. A shallow, grassy slope led to the train platform. Lines had formed and there was no pushing or shoving. No doubt having Mrs. Umbra, the exceedingly intimidating head of dark magic overseeing things explained everyone's patience.

Dean Blane had arranged a compartment for them in the rear car so Conryu's mom could continue her work. Lucky for them, the first cars were being loaded first so they didn't have to wait in line. They reached the door and were preparing to board when the rune stone in her pocket grew warm.

Maria scrambled to pull it out without breaking the spell holding Mrs. Koda's gear. "Conryu? Are you okay? I tried to contact you, but nothing happened. Yes, I'm perfectly calm. You were in the Black City for a personal meeting with the Reaper? Okay. Look, Atlantis has attacked Jemma's school and they're on their way here. No, we're fine and on our way out. If you have weapons, help Jemma first. Yes, I'm sure. Your mother's fine. She's with me now. Okay, see you soon."

"He's okay?" Mrs. Koda asked.

"Yeah, he just got out of a meeting with the ruler of Hell. But for Conryu, that's less strange than it sounds." Maria climbed the steps, carefully maneuvering the workbench through the narrow door. "Hopefully he can help Jemma and the students over there."

"And while he's doing it, I'll finish my bomb so we can blow them back to wherever they came from."

---

Jemma risked a look behind her. Smoke rose from the school grounds and the sounds of gunfire had largely fallen silent. The soldiers had lasted longer than she'd feared, but not nearly long enough.

She ducked a tree branch and hurried on. Ahead of her, fifty students and six teachers fled on foot through the woods surrounding the grounds. Hopefully soon they'd reach the edge of the anti-magic field. She felt weak and exposed without her magic.

Not that it was much good against these crystal monsters. At least it made her feel less helpless, and more importantly, they could escape. She understood better now that nowhere was safe, but nowhere she could think of was less safe than here.

Something exploded ahead of them and flames shot toward the sky.

Students screamed.

Jemma ran forward past huddled young people. When she reached the front of the group she found a smoking hole. The crystal ship floated about fifty yards above them, a larger protrusion at the front pointing down at the woods.

One of the teachers, a new one that looked like she'd been a student the year before, said in a trembling voice, "Anna was in the lead. The blast hit her…"

Jemma got the picture. A blast that big must have taken a lot of power. They needed to move before it recharged.

"Get everyone going. Tell them to spread out."

The teacher nodded and hurried back, urging everyone to get up. Jemma needed to distract that ship so her people could escape, but how, she couldn't even throw rocks at the damn thing.

As she was thinking, the protrusion started to glow. Jemma waved at it and ran left. Maybe movement would draw it. It wasn't like she had any better ideas.

When the blast came, it struck behind her.

Jemma went flying, slammed into a tree trunk, and slid down.

She groaned and winced. It felt like a few of her ribs had broken.

The crystal ship swung away. It was getting ready to target more of her students.

Jemma raised a weak hand, but there was nothing she could do.

She rolled over on her back. Something rustled and a moment later one of the crystal monsters stepped out from behind a pair of saplings.

It pointed at her and the tip of its finger started to glow.

This was it.

She closed her eyes.

A loud crunch was followed by a dull thud.

Jemma opened her eyes and found a woman in all black standing over the prone form of her would-be killer. The ninja held an odd weapon of black steel with a spike on one side. Whatever it was, it had killed the Atlantean soldier.

"Are you all right?" the ninja asked.

"No, but I'll live, thanks to you."

The woman shook her head. "The Chosen bade us save as many of you as we could. It is him you must thank."

Conryu, of course. "Where is he and how did you get here so fast?"

"The anti-magic field only extends five hundred feet from that ship in a dome below it. We appeared at its edge and ran. As for the Chosen, he is up there, dealing with the leader of this force."

Conryu landed lightly on the deck of the crystal ship and Kai joined him an instant later. For this fight, he'd placed Prime in the pocket dimension where he kept the Staff of All Elements. The scholomantic wasn't thrilled, but without magic to protect him, Prime was too easy of a target.

He tightened his grip on his weapon. The Hell-forged mace was heavy in his hand, but not in a bad way. It was incredibly reassuring to finally have a way of defeating these crystal monsters. Hopefully the other ninjas weren't having too much trouble with the ones on the ground.

At the front of the ship stood a more refined crystal person, a man this time, who could have been the brother of the woman they fought on the floating island. He stared at them as if not fully comprehending what he was seeing. Though it was hard to say for sure given his total lack of expression.

Perhaps he hadn't realized the weakness in his defense. The anti-magic field that protected the ship only extended six feet above the deck. Conryu had simply opened the library doors at its edge and then jumped down. Nothing to it really. This was where the challenge really began.

The crystal man pointed at Conryu and loosed a beam of crimson energy.

He dodged and Kai charged. The plan was for whoever didn't get attacked to close and bring the Reaper's weapon to bear.

Their opponent thrust his open palm at Kai and sent her flying backward.

Conryu grimaced and made his own attack.

Only fifty feet separated him from the crystal man, but it might as well have been a mile. He only made it halfway before another shockwave sent him tumbling ass over elbows across the deck.

Kai had regained her feet and made it within fifteen feet before cartwheeling out of the way of a crimson ray.

Conryu raced to join her.

When the shockwave came, he was ready. He caught Kai in midair, spun her around, and hurled her back at the crystal man.

The enemy didn't have time to respond before her mace crashed into his head. Cracks appeared in his cheek, but the spike didn't penetrate deeply enough to kill him.

The Atlantean staggered back.

Kai lashed out again, but this time he was ready. Her opponent caught the haft of her mace with one hand and pointed at her with the other.

An instant before the crimson ray could fire, Conryu slammed his own mace into the Atlantean's wrist. The beam burned a line down the deck but missed Kai by a good half a foot.

Conryu spun and hammered the spike into the Atlantean's chest. He'd hit concrete softer than that crystal. He barely penetrated an eighth of an inch.

He staggered back another step and Kai freed her weapon from his grasp.

"Kai, double impact."

Hopefully she'd get what he meant. Conryu stepped in and swung with all his might.

The tip of his mace hit hard but failed to penetrate. An instant later Kai struck his mace with the blunt end of her weapon. Crystal cracked as the spike broke through. Liquid darkness surged into the Atlantean, blotting out the golden mist that had filled his body.

An ear-splitting wail filled the air before the crystal man fell forward and shattered on the deck.

"Are you okay?" Kai asked.

Conryu nodded. He was better than okay. His magic had returned and they now knew that the Reaper's weapons were effective against the Atlanteans.

"Let's see if anyone was hurt on the ground." Conryu stood beside Kai and activated a flying spell. They soared down from the ship which appeared content to just float where it was.

The trees here weren't especially thick and he soon spotted one of the ninjas standing beside Jemma who was lying on the ground propped up by a tree.

They landed and the ninja bowed. "Is it done, Chosen?"

"Yeah." Conryu knelt beside Jemma and sent light magic into her, mending broken ribs and closing some small internal ruptures. A few seconds later he helped her to her feet. "Better?"

"Much, thank you." Jemma looked up at the immobile

crystal ship. "You defeated the Atlantean without magic. How?"

Conryu held up his mace. "A gift from the Reaper himself. I'm glad it worked. Your people?"

"I'm not sure. When the ship fired on us, we got separated. I tried to draw its fire but ran into a crystal monster. I thought I was dead, but your friend here saved my life."

Conryu grinned. "You can always count on a ninja when you're in trouble."

He held out a fist to the woman who stared at it in confusion. Kai whispered to her and she finally bumped fists with him. They might be lethal, but they'd been pretty isolated for a long time.

Another ninja appeared out of the borderland. She pulled her mask down. It was Kanna. "Chosen, the enemy continues to fight, but they do so in an aimless fashion. With our powers working it's only a matter of time before we've defeated them. What do you wish us to do next?"

He looked to Jemma. "Do you need help finding or healing your staff and students?"

"No, once the threat is eliminated, we can round everyone up and see to their injuries. Do you have a plan for dealing with Atlantis itself?"

"Sort of." Conryu was mindful of the Reaper's command not to mention the secret power source. "We need to destroy all the Atlanteans as well as a huge crystal in the center of the city called the Heart of Atlantis. I have an idea about how to get in, but smashing a giant crystal, even with Hell-forged weapons, isn't going to be an easy task. Before any of that, we've got to deal with the second ship and its passengers. Kanna, finish up here and we'll head out."

She bowed and disappeared to carry out his orders. Now that he knew what they were dealing with, Conryu was more eager than ever to get back to Maria.

## CHAPTER 25

When they reached Atlantis, Merik was stuck once again in the apartment prison they'd prepared for him. The tedious, empty waiting could drive a man to drink, if there was anything to drink in this place besides water. This time, even Tanidel hadn't bothered to pretend they cared what he had to say.

He was too human for the inhuman Atlanteans. At least that was the impression he got. They didn't trust him and the feeling was mutual. All he could think about was when they were going to trigger the crystal in his head and turn him into a mindless slave like the cultists. That they hadn't yet argued that some shred of humanity remained in them, but it was a small shred.

He rolled over on his hard, crystal bed, trying to get comfortable. It was futile so he swung his legs over the edge and sat up.

Out of nowhere, a jagged pain stabbed into his brain. It was gone as quickly as it appeared, but his central crystal remained vibrating.

Something had happened and he doubted it was good. Merik needed answers and he was going to get them, assuming he could escape this room.

He marched over to the spot in front of the wall where the door appeared and concentrated. Come on, goddamn it! He was of Atlantean blood. No stupid wall was going to keep him from finding out what was going on.

His staring contest with the wall had gone on long enough for him to feel foolish when a ripple ran through the crystal and the door opened.

Merik leapt out into the hall before the wall changed its mind. He found the stairs down easily enough and soon reached the wall that led to the lobby. This time he got the door to open after only a few seconds of staring. Maybe he was getting better at it.

The meeting room where he first encountered the survivors was empty. He scratched his jaw. The city was a big place, they could be anywhere. The only place he could think to start was the giant red crystal Tanidel had showed him just before Atlantis returned to the human realm. If they were doing something that caused his pain, that would be where they did it.

Outside, all the crystal streets looked the same. He set out in what he thought was the right direction. Merik debated trying to reach out through his connection to Tanidel but decided against it. With the way the others had been acting lately, he'd lost a lot of faith in them. Better to find his way on his own.

Walking through the empty streets, Merik felt like an archeologist in an adventure movie exploring some lost civilization. It took a while, but he finally rounded a bend and spotted the red crystal. As he thought, the others were gathered nearby.

He took a step then hesitated. Faced with the reality before him, demanding answers suddenly didn't seem like the wisest decision. Before he could make up his mind, one of them pointed at the ground beside the crystal. An opening appeared and they descended out of sight.

The idea of sub-levels never occurred to him. What could they have down there? Caution and curiosity warred within him.

Curiosity won.

He tiptoed across the park and peered down into the hole. It was lit with glowing crystals much like the cave where Merik found the key. The familiarity of it reassured him and he stepped on the first stair.

No reaction.

He blew out a sigh and started down. The staircase spiraled ever deeper. He had lost track of how many paces he'd taken when he heard voices. The words were indistinct, but they were definitely speaking. But to who?

The Atlanteans could converse mind to mind so there had to be someone else.

Merik slowed his approach, cautious now as the voices grew louder. An archway at the base of the stairs led to a huge, domed cavern. In the center, the Atlanteans were gathered around a pillar of flickering darkness. He couldn't make out exactly what the darkness was, but it looked like flames, if flames came in black. The flames rose out of a circular pit in the center of the floor and vanished into the ceiling.

"One of our brothers has died," a deep male voice said. "You said the battle would be easily won."

"No." The reply seemed to come from the middle of the flames. "I said the battle was winnable. Did you think the wizards would simply lie down and let you slaughter them? People die in war. It is unavoidable. That one of you has fallen is unfortunate, but did you truly imagine that you would emerge from a battle with the entire world unscathed? Especially when you rushed into it against my advice."

"We had no choice," the Atlantean representative countered. "Once the city was discovered, we needed to put them on the defensive. If we hadn't, the city itself might have come under attack."

"So? With your defenses, any attack would have been doomed before it got close. Your fear is what got your brother killed, not any promise I made. Now, what is it you wish of me? I've given you all the power I can so all I have left to offer is advice, though I doubt you'll heed me."

"We will," Tanidel said. "Please, what should we do?"

"It's difficult now that your enemy knows your capabilities. Some of you must go forth to gather more soldiers. It will be a trial to remain undetected, but you have no other choice. Once you have an unstoppable army, then make your move against the larger cities. Don't focus on the wizards, just kill them as you can. My final word of advice is that you deal with the snoop spying on us. He's clearly not committed."

All the Atlanteans turned toward Merik. He thought to run, but where could he go on a floating island? Instead he stepped out into the cavern. "A strange pain struck me. I came looking for you to see what it was. I'm sorry for the death of your friend."

"You should have stayed in your room," Tanidel said.

"I will not be a prisoner here." Merik glared at them. "Since we returned, I've gone from savior of Atlantis to prisoner of Atlantis. I don't like that a bit. Either tell me what's going on or take me back to Ireland. I can find my way home from there."

It was a pretty good speech even if he did say so himself.

He barely finished congratulating himself when his body

went rigid and he fell to the floor. A moment later he floated up and over to the others.

"It's unfortunate you chose not to dedicate yourself fully to the mission," Tanidel said. "Since we can't risk you interfering, you will remain here while we complete our work. When it's finished, you will be free to live the rest of your life as we agreed."

He wanted to snarl and ask what sort of world he'd be living in, one surrounded by crystal people, a lone human in a land of living statues. Unfortunately, his mouth was as rigid as the rest of his body.

Merik floated up a few feet from the pillar of black flame. The others filed out, leaving him alone with whatever lived in the fire. He wasn't eager to get better acquainted.

When Angus and Sienna arrived at the Central train station, they were promptly told that there were no trains to the Academy scheduled in the near future. That was disappointing but he was hardly shocked. Luckily, while she wasn't able to open a portal, Sienna was powerful enough to cast Fly on both of them.

Which was how Angus found himself soaring just above the treetops toward the Academy. They were certain to attract attention, but he was confident he could talk the teachers out of killing them on the spot. While most of them liked him no better than Conryu did, he was known to be friendly.

"What's going on down there?" Sienna asked.

Angus frowned and looked where she pointed. It appeared as though the entire school was preparing to board a train. "I think they're evacuating. Perhaps our warning will prove unnecessary."

They dove toward the gathering. Angus winced and said a silent prayer that no one attacked. God must have been watching over them. They landed twenty yards from the collected students.

"Where is the girlfriend?" Sienna asked.

Angus didn't see Maria, but she could have boarded already. He did see the withered, black-robed figure of Angeline Umbra shuffling their way.

"As always," Angeline said. "Your timing is horrendous. It's almost bad enough to be an actual curse. What do you want and who is your friend?"

"We have no time to waste." Sienna tried to push past Angeline and got a thump with the Death Stick for her trouble. She collapsed in a limp heap.

Angeline quirked an eyebrow. "Well?"

"It's a long story. We're trying to get in touch with Conryu. His mother wasn't home, so I figured Maria was the next best option. I assume you know about Atlantis."

"I know they've attacked our sister school in the Kingdom and that there's another ship on the way here. It's still a ways out so the boy went to help Jemma. His mother's here, working on some kind of weapon she thinks can destroy the crystal people using technology instead of magic. I didn't understand half of what she described, but the dean seemed confident. Who's the young idiot?"

"Her name's Sienna and she's part of a long line of wizards whose duty it was to stop the return of Atlantis. She seemed to think you needed to know what she had to say, but it sounds like you're pretty well up to speed."

Angeline grunted. "If I let her move, she's not going to do something else stupid is she?"

"I don't believe so. We aren't especially well acquainted."

She tapped Sienna on the arm and she scrambled to her

feet. She glared daggers at Angeline, but the head of dark magic didn't seem terribly impressed.

A piercing whistle broke the tension. Dean Blane was waving at them. "The ship has picked up speed. We need to go."

Angeline waved back. "You two had best come along. Unless you want to wait for a shipload of crystal monsters to arrive."

"What sort of crystal monsters?" Sienna asked as they walked toward the train.

"Humanoid, around seven feet tall, made of jagged crystal. They seem to be able to use a heat ray as well as some sort of repulsion spell. And they're totally immune to direct magical attacks."

"Atlantean soldier drones," Sienna said as much to herself as to them. "They've already begun converting ordinary humans."

"What?" Converting humans didn't sound good.

"They developed the technique late in the war to increase their numbers. If they're using it from the start, then there can't be many actual Atlanteans in the city. That is excellent news."

"Angus." Dean Blane nodded at him as they boarded the train. "Find an empty seat, we're leaving now."

There was one seat left in the car they entered forcing Angus and Sienna to squeeze in together. Ordinarily being in such close proximity to an attractive young woman would have been something he enjoyed, but with the threat of an imminent attack, he was too tense.

The train lurched and they were underway. All around them the girls were murmuring in soft voices. He picked out few words, but the general tone was one of anxiety. Angus knew his history pretty well, but he couldn't recall the Academy ever having to be evacuated.

"Again my efforts come to nothing," Sienna muttered.

"What?"

"They already know everything. Neither my warning nor help are needed. I might better have stayed in the Kingdom and helped them fight the crystal soldiers."

"It's the thought that counts," Angus said.

She looked at him and he had to admit that sounded pretty pathetic. Her eyes widened.

"What is it?"

"I sense Atlantean magic. Where is that hag? The enemy is close."

Calling Angeline a hag probably wasn't wise if you wanted to live a long, healthy life, but now wasn't the time to discuss it. He stood, but there were only young people in every direction.

An explosion sounded somewhere ahead of them, rocking the train.

"The track!" one of the girls in a window seat screamed. "Something blew up the tracks!"

## CHAPTER 26

Conryu was in the middle of healing a water aligned student when the buzz from Maria's rune stone tickled his brain. He initiated contact at once.
"Maria?"

"The Atlanteans destroyed a section of track and we can't stop the train in time. Hurry."

He didn't need to hear anything else. The girl he was healing was out of danger.

Two steps away from her he opened a Hell gate and vanished. With time basically stopped he had a moment to think. Cerberus whined and butted his arm with his central head. Conryu absently scratched it.

Stopping the train would be impossible with the time the and distance available. He couldn't bring them here; it would kill Maria. A wind or Heaven portal were his only options.

He leapt onto Cerberus's back. "Take me to the Academy train."

The demon dog leapt at his command. Kai could catch up on her own. He didn't have time to waste.

*Stopping Atlantis is your priority, not saving a few wizards.*

"I'm not letting Maria and my mother die. We already killed one of the crystal people. Kanna and the others are hunting down any strays. Now be quiet and let me concentrate. Once they're safe I'll get back to your war."

A forbidding power filled the air around him. Conryu ignored the implied threat. The Reaper needed him to seal the void rift. He might complain, but until that was done, the lord of Hell wouldn't lash out. Afterwards, well, he'd deal with afterwards later.

Cerberus stopped and Conryu opened a viewing window. Directly ahead of them was the train. He shifted his view and found a crater in the middle of where the track was supposed to run. If the train hit that it would kill or hurt hundreds. He had about fifty yards to open the portal. Even for him, that would be tight.

His mace would be useless for this, so he swapped it for the staff and hopped down from Cerberus's back. "Wish me luck."

Cerberus barked and Conryu emerged into the real world directly in the path of a racing train. He leveled the staff and commanded a Heaven gate to open. A white disk appeared and expanded nearly as fast as the nose of the train.

The magic levitation train didn't have conventional brakes and so could do little to slow itself in a hurry.

Conryu poured more of his will into the staff.

With three yards to spare, the portal grew large enough to accept the train. It vanished into the whiteness and Conryu followed, closing the gate behind him.

Ahead of him, the train continued to race away. Fortunately, Heaven was infinite and he had all the time in the world to stop it. Not that he planned to dawdle.

"I hate it here," Prime said.

"I know, but until everyone's safe you'll have to bear it."

Conryu closed his eyes and reached out to the golden lions that guarded the gates of Heaven. "I could use a hand, guys."

With his request sent, he willed himself after the retreating train. It took only a moment to catch up. As he flew along the caboose, he saw his mother staring out a window with wide eyes. Maria was in the next window looking every bit as impressed. Conryu was pretty sure he'd brought Maria to Heaven at least once, but a lot had happened and he couldn't actually remember.

A golden glow racing in from the left drew him away. As he got closer, the light resolved itself into a golden lion every bit as big as Cerberus.

"Can you help me stop the train?"

The lion roared and leapt in front of the train. It reached out with paws bigger than Conryu's chest and caught the engine. It wasn't a gentle stop, but after another fifty yards it was still.

Conryu flew over and patted its flank. "Thanks. I'll get everyone out of your hair as soon as I can."

The lion purred for a moment then glared at Prime who huddled behind Conryu's shoulder. With that parting warning to the demon book, the lion rocketed back the way it had come.

"I don't like those beasts either," Prime said.

"It appears mutual. Come on, let's make sure everyone is okay."

They flew to the caboose and Conryu slid the door open. Maria rushed out and hugged him. "I thought we were dead."

Conryu sighed and held her for a moment. "I'm surprised one of the teachers didn't open a portal themselves."

There was a snort behind him. He let Maria go and turned to find Mrs. Umbra flying their way.

"I doubt all the light aligned teachers working together

could open a portal big enough for the train to pass through," she said. "Certainly not in the amount of time we had. We hoped to escape the Atlanteans and instead drove right into their sights. Not our best decision."

"You couldn't have known," Conryu said.

"Hello, dear." His mother was standing in the caboose door with a bemused look on her face. "Is this...?"

"Heaven, yeah. The outskirts anyway. Are you okay, Mom?" He flew closer and hugged her.

"I'm fine. Is your father..."

"I'm sure he's up here somewhere, but the souls of the dead are kept behind Heaven's gates. No living people allowed."

Her expression nearly broke his heart. "I would have liked to see him."

"Me too." He squeezed her tighter.

When he finally let her go, an unwelcome voice said, "Conryu, my boy. I might have known it was you that saved us."

Ignoring Angus for the moment he asked his mother, "What's he doing here?"

"I didn't know he was. I've been focused on my sonic bomb."

"Sonic bomb?"

"Yes, I thought it would be the best way to shatter crystal. It has a control panel to match the vibration of the explosion to that of the target." She touched the tip of her chin, lost in thought. "I'm not sure it would be of much use in combat, too slow and unwieldly. My next move is to miniaturize it. Turn it into a grenade. The trick is matching the target vibration. I haven't worked that out yet."

"I'm sure you will, Mom. But in the meantime, I'm going to need your big bomb."

"What for, dear?"

"To blow up the Heart of Atlantis."

"Conryu," Angus said in a more insistent tone. "We really need to talk. Please."

Clearly, he was going to get no peace until he heard the pain in the neck out. When he faced Angus this time, a young woman stood beside him. It wasn't one of the students, she wasn't dressed in a school robe. Of course, that begged the question of who she was.

"What?" Conryu asked.

"I want you to meet Sienna." Angus nodded toward the woman. "She's descended from the people of Lemuria, Atlantis's sworn enemy. She has information that can help."

Conryu met Sienna's gaze. Her blue-green eyes were hard and focused, a warrior's eyes. "I'm listening."

"You know of the floating island falling out of the sky?" When he nodded she said, "They did that. Madagascar was the Lemurian homeland in ancient times. It's possible they plan to bring down more of them."

"They did," Conryu said. "Kai and I destroyed the devices they used to negate the island's magic. Unless they have more of them hidden somewhere, no more islands will be falling from the sky."

She flinched back, clearly surprised that he already knew. "You've encountered the Atlanteans?"

"Yeah. They're made of crystal, immune to magic, and tough as hell. It was all Kai and I could do to kill one of them. I don't know how many are left, but we're in for a fight, that's for sure."

"You defeated one of them in combat?" She was staring at him now the way people used to look when they first learned there was a male wizard. "How could you have accomplished more in days than I have in my entire life?"

"I had help. Listen, if there's nothing else, I need to talk to Dean Blane and figure out where we're going to take everyone so they'll be safe until Atlantis is dealt with. Excuse me."

He barely turned his back on them when the Goddess's gentle voice appeared in his mind. *There is a matter we must discuss.*

Why was he so bloody popular all of a sudden? He sensed her location and sighed. The students would be safe enough until he got back. It wasn't polite to leave a goddess waiting.

---

Conryu flew through Heaven's endless clouds until the train was out of sight. The Goddess was close. It seemed she didn't want to be seen by the others for some reason. He shrugged, shot through a cloud, and there she was. Dressed all in white, a golden aura surrounding her, the Goddess was life and beauty personified, the polar opposite of the Reaper. If he had to be summoned by someone, he'd much rather it be her.

He bowed and offered his best smile. "Sorry about the train. I wasn't sure where else to bring them."

"It is of no concern," she said. "I must speak to you of Atlantis."

"I was afraid of that. The Reaper told me about the void power they tapped into and about the war with Lemuria. Is there more?"

"I'm sure he told you what he thought you needed to know. What I want to add may not be truly relevant to the current situation, but I wanted to share it anyway. You see, the war began before the Atlanteans broke through reality into the void. They turned to that power in desperation. My followers urged the others to sue for peace before it came to that, but we were outvoted. Lemuria was winning, they said. Why offer peace when victory was close?"

"He neglected to mention that, which is no surprise. I'm not thrilled about having to wipe out the last remnants of a race, but from what I've seen, any humanity they might have had is long gone. If you have another option, I'm all ears. Otherwise…"

Her glowing eyes clouded and her expression grew sad. "No. Much as I might wish it were otherwise, there are no other options. The power of the void is too dangerous to leave unchecked. I am sorry this burden falls to you. It's hardly fair, but you were chosen for moments like this."

"There's one thing that's bothering me. What happens to Atlantis itself after I seal the rift?"

"You will have to shift it into a pocket dimension. It will be safe there until the hole in our reality is fully healed. Don't worry, when the time comes, we will guide you through the process." She leaned forward and kissed his forehead. "Good luck and be careful, my Chosen. Though they are much diminished, the Atlanteans are still a formidable threat."

He bowed once more and when he straightened, she was gone.

"What now, Master?" Prime asked.

"Now we get everyone home and plan our attack."

## CHAPTER 27

At Dean Blane's insistence, Conryu brought them back in a secluded place on the West Coast. It was beautiful, with a log cabin, fields and mountains all around, but there was no way everyone would fit in that one lodge. When he pointed this out, she assured him that by the end of the day, everyone would be distributed across the country to make them more difficult targets.

He was just closing the Heaven gate when Kai appeared beside him. "What happened? You vanished without a word and I couldn't find you."

"There was an emergency." He gave her the short version of what happened. "I didn't intend to worry you. Did you guys finish up the crystal soldiers?"

"Yes, without a leader, defeating them was not difficult. We are ready to strike Atlantis on your command."

"Good. I have a few details to clear up then we'll go. I don't want to give them any more time to prepare than necessary."

Kai nodded once and vanished back into the borderlands.

Maria, Dean Blane, his mother, Angus, and the new girl, Sienna, were standing in a circle around a box about two feet square. That had to be the sonic bomb his mother mentioned. Hopefully it wouldn't be too difficult to use. He made the short walk to join them.

Before he could speak Maria said, "If you're going to attack Atlantis, I'm coming with you."

"As am I," Sienna added. "It is my duty to put right my mistake."

He glanced at Dean Blane, but she didn't make an announcement about her intentions. "Actually, I was hoping to get a group of six or so light magic users to oversee a medical station where Kai and her sisters could retreat for healing. If you want to be in charge of that, Maria, it would be a huge help."

Maria positively beamed at the idea. "Healing's my best subject. I can totally handle that. I'll go ask for volunteers."

"Feel free to ask the light aligned teachers as well," Dean Blane said.

Conryu turned to Sienna. "As for you, if you wish to come, I don't mind. I'd offer you an extra Hell-forged mace, but it would probably melt your hands off."

"I've never wielded a mace anyway," Sienna said.

Finally he focused on the sonic bomb. "Okay, Mom. Show me how this thing works."

Conryu's plan to approach Atlantis was very similar to his plan when he and Kai attacked the crystal ship. They'd approach from below, out of sight, getting as close as the anti-magic field would allow, then fire grappling hooks into the stone below the city. After that it was just a matter of climbing and fighting until they reached the Heart of Atlantis.

He shook his head. If only it was that easy.

The library, stuffed to the brim with ninjas, was in place beneath Atlantis. They'd been able to get closer than he'd feared. The bottom of the stone was only a couple hundred feet above the door. A tough climb but doable. Now they just needed to wait for Jemma's distraction.

He checked his phone. The first strikes should hit any moment now. "Are the launchers ready, Kanna?"

"Yes, Chosen." He'd asked three times already, but her tone held no sign of annoyance.

"Okay." He moved out of the doorway and willed it wider so all ten ninjas could stand side by side. "Move them into position."

The launchers were basically tubes that held a grappling hook and had an explosive charge at the rear. The army guy they got them from assured Conryu that they could fire three hundred yards easy. That was way more than they needed, but better too much than not enough.

He checked the time again. Thirty seconds, assuming they were on time.

A moment later he heard the distant roar of jet engines.

This was it. "Everyone ready."

The launchers went up into position.

When the first explosion sounded, he said, "Fire!"

As one they hit the triggers and sent their grappling hooks soaring toward the edge of the city. They cleared easily. Everyone hauled their ropes back until they caught. Two came clattering back over the edge, having failed to hook an outcropping. It didn't matter. Eight would be enough.

"Go, go, go!"

He grabbed the nearest rope, but Kanna caught his shoulder. "We will secure the entry point, Chosen. You come up with the second wave."

He grimaced but nodded. Sending people into danger ahead of him wasn't Conryu's style, but he was the only one that could seal the void rift. If he fell before he completed his mission, that threat would remain, maybe forever. That wasn't an outcome he could risk.

The ninjas climbed the ropes in seconds. On the opposite side of the city, RAF jets continued to pound away, though their missiles all slammed into an invisible barrier and detonated without doing any damage. As long as they kept the Atlanteans' focus away from them, Conryu didn't care what else the pilots did.

The first wave reached the top and after an agonizing half minute one of them waved the all clear signal. Conryu began his climb with Kai right beside him. He was honest enough to admit he'd lost a little fitness since gaining his magical abilities, but he still made the top without stopping to rest. Carrying a pack with his mother's sonic bomb inside didn't make it any easier.

As soon as he arrived, he moved aside to let the next group come aboard. As he fought to regain his breath he took in the view. Atlantis was a stunning place. Crystal towers filled the skyline. Even the streets were paved with crystal. Only the occasional park or tree broke up the endless expanse of shining, clear crystal. It was so alien he couldn't begin to imagine how one would go about building such a place.

"You could probably do it with earth magic if you really wanted to," Prime said.

He certainly didn't want to. The next group arrived meaning they had a third of their force in place. They could at least start scouting around. The Heart would naturally be in the center, or so he assumed.

Just to be sure he turned to Sienna. "Where will we find the Heart?"

"I have no idea." Her dark skin was so pale he feared she might faint. "No Lemurian has ever set foot in Atlantis proper."

So much for their expert. "Kanna, send out some scouts to have a look around. If they don't know we're here, they will soon. I don't want to be taken by surprise."

She nodded, pointed at one group of four, and pointed east. Another group went west, and a third went straight down the street they were standing on.

While they scouted Conryu paced. There had to be some sort of defenses beyond the towers and their crimson rays. Guards, golems, something.

His cellphone buzzed, distracting him from his worries. "Jemma? How long? Okay, thanks."

He disconnected and Kanna and Kai both looked at him. "The crystal ship is on its way back and it's going like crazy. Jemma says we've got maybe an hour to finish our business before we'll have an army of crystal soldiers breathing down our neck. I know we planned to take our time, but that's out the window now. Get everyone up here as fast as you can. We're making a run for the city center."

Walking through the empty city may have been the tensest thing Conryu had ever done. Every moment he expected something to attack them. Once one of the towers lit up and he feared they were about to get blasted to ash. Instead in shot a beam at one of the fighters still buzzing around outside. The crystal towers would have made perfect perches for snipers, but none made themselves known. In fact, Conryu didn't see so much as a door to get into the towers. Was it possible they were used strictly for external defense? He didn't know. There was so much he didn't know it was making him crazy.

When a pair of ninjas came running toward them, he

welcomed the distraction. A moment later he frowned. They worked in groups of four, so where were the other two?

Kanna must have read his mind. "Where are your squadmates?"

"Gone to the aid station," one of them said. "We found the enemy. Ten of the crystal people are gathered in a park. They have taken up defensive positions around a crimson crystal twice as big as one of our huts. When we tried to sneak in for a closer look, they spotted us and loosed one of those red beams. It singed Arie's ribs so Kay helped her escape while we reported back."

Conryu relaxed a fraction. At least no one was badly injured. "The crystal people, were they smooth or jagged?"

"Smooth, like glass," the ninja said.

Ten of the stronger ones, great. "Call everyone back. I need to get something from the library."

Kai followed him as he ran back the way they'd come. "What do you need, Chosen?"

"Shields. Without some sort of protection, those crimson rays will cut us to shreds."

Kai gave him a curious look. "Do you have shields in the library?"

"No, but I can make them if I get somewhere magic works."

Conryu ended up having to travel to the realm of earth to forge his shields. A pair of helpful elementals were kind enough to point him in the direction of a special metal that was highly resistant to heat. He made ten tall, wide shields with it. Now all he had to do was hope that the crimson rays were actually heat based.

The ninjas were gathered at the edge of where the Heart

sat. He'd never seen a crystal that big and even from a distance he could feel it pulsing with power. In front of him, Kanna grasped the shield with both hands. They had turned out heavier than he'd wanted, but if they held up, he didn't care. They just needed to force their way through to the crystal then make a wall so he could set the sonic bomb.

"I don't know about this, Chosen," Kanna said. "We're not used to fighting with shields."

"You're not fighting with them now. Think of them as mobile barriers. Once we close in, you can ditch them and fight the way you usually do. Just remember what I told you about the crystal people."

"We will keep their toughness in mind, rest assured." Kanna looked around. "I believe everyone is ready."

Conryu tightened his grip on his mace. "Give the signal."

She made a chopping motion toward the Atlanteans and all ten groups surged forward.

A lance of crimson light shot out and struck the shield of the group to their right. The shield took the hit, turning orange in the center, before quickly cooling.

Conryu grinned. He owned those elementals a glass of whatever they liked to drink, assuming they drank anything.

His happiness lasted only a moment. A deep thrum filled the air and one of the rows of ninjas was sent flying back across the lawn.

They had switched to the low vibration attack he thought of as a battering ram. Against that the shields were worthless.

"Faster, Kanna. We need to close before they hit us with one of those."

She picked up the pace. Any moment he expected to be sent flying.

More of the battering ram attacks struck home, sending

ninjas flying in all directions. The women quickly scrambled to their feet to avoid the crimson rays that followed.

Kanna peeked around the edge of the shield. "We're getting close."

The words had barely left her mouth when a battering ram struck them.

Kanna, Conryu, Kai, and the woman behind her were sent flying. He landed hard, rolled to his feet, and scrambled for the shield.

Kanna was lying still, half under its bulk.

He ran over and picked it up just in time to intercept a ray.

Kai sprinted over beside him.

"Is she okay?" he asked.

"Yes, just knocked out."

The clash of steel on crystal filled the air. One of the teams had made contact with the Atlanteans. They were going to need backup and fast.

"We have to leave her," he said. A small group of the least experienced ninjas was on recovery duty. They'd see that Kanna made it to healers. "Let's go. Prime, I want you to keep an eye out and let me know if one of the Atlanteans targets us. When they do, we break and charge together."

"Yes, Master," Prime said.

"Understood." Kai gave a final look back at Kanna then shifted to get behind him.

Conryu marched forward as fast as he could without losing his balance with the heavy shield. They were three-quarters of the way back to where they first got hit when Prime said, "Now, Master."

He hurled the shield forward with all his might then darted right. Kai went left at the same time.

They both made it out of the way seconds before the shield

came flying back through the space they just vacated. That was their cue to charge.

He reached the female Atlantean just as she pointed at Kai. A hard blow of his mace drove her arm out to the side and the crimson ray streaked out four feet wide of its target.

Kai never slowed. Five feet out she leapt and drove the spike of her mace right between the woman's eyes.

Conryu didn't wait to see the result.

He hammered the back of her mace a second time, driving the spike in deeper.

Darkness oozed out, devouring the golden glow swirling through the Atlantean's crystal body.

For an instant, the destruction of their comrade caused the others to flinch.

It wasn't much of an opening, but it was enough for the Daughters. Dozens of trained killers fell on the Atlanteans, hammering them without mercy.

A battering ram thrummed, sending a handful of ninjas flying. Two Atlanteans fled.

A minute later the park was silent. Lifeless crystal statues lay scattered around. A few black-clad bodies were mixed in, but far fewer than he'd feared. Hopefully they were only hurt, but deep down Conryu knew there was no way they'd escaped this fight with no deaths. Life just didn't work that way.

While the recovery team saw to those that had fallen, the rest of the ninja gathered around Conryu. "Orders, Chosen?" one of them asked.

"Everyone get back while I set the sonic bomb. Assuming it works, we still need to track down those final Atlanteans."

He shrugged out of his pack and pulled out the device his mother had built. It looked like something from a hundred years ago, with wires sticking up and a pair of dials on the face.

The only modern part was a digital readout it looked like she stole from a cellphone.

Conryu placed the bomb tight against the red crystal like he was told and twisted the right-hand dial. Two lines appeared on the screen, one wavy and the other straight. Gradually the straight one bent until it matched the wavy one. He turned the left-hand dial until the number sixty appeared below the lines. He released the knob and the countdown began.

## CHAPTER 28

The sonic bomb didn't exactly explode. Instead it let out this deep thud, that compressed his chest and made Conryu's heart skip a beat. The explosion came an instant later when the crystal blew into a million tiny pieces that then rained down on him and the ninjas. The pieces were light, but razor sharp. There were a few minor cuts, but nothing serious.

As soon as the crystal had burst, Conryu's connection to magic returned. A quick pulse of light magic healed him and everyone around him of their injuries.

"We need to find the survivors," he said. "Don't let them get out of the city."

The ninjas vanished into the borderland to begin their hunt leaving Conryu, Kai, and Sienna alone in the park. It wouldn't take the others long to hunt down the escapees. He needed to figure out where this void rift was and seal it. The fewer people that knew about it, the better.

Conryu walked to the edge of where the destroyed crystal had sat and stared at the hole left behind. Below the park was a massive cavern. It was so dark and so far down he couldn't make out any detail. That said, it certainly seemed like a good place to put something you wanted to hide.

He swapped his mace for his staff, touched Kai's arm, and activated a flying spell. The masters of the elemental realms probably wouldn't be thrill that he was bringing her all, but Conryu didn't care. He'd need backup just in case there was a problem.

Before he could warn Sienna off, she leapt over the edge and glided down out of sight. She'd collected one of the fallen maces and still had both of her hands. She must have known a defensive spell that worked. He wasn't about to turn down the extra help and at this point what was one more person in on the secret? She'd been mixed up in this craziness since the beginning. She had a right to see it to the end.

"Ready?" he asked.

Kai nodded and they flew down after Sienna. Halfway down he conjured lights and scattered them throughout the cavern. The glowing spheres revealed a flat, smooth disk of darkness with a man standing in front of it. Not a crystal man, but a flesh-and-blood human. Albeit one with crystals stuck in his forehead and eyes as black as the rift behind him.

Sienna stood facing the man, her mace cocked and ready like she planned to bash his brains in any second.

As if reading his mind, she launched herself at the stranger and swung hard enough that the tendons in her neck stood out.

The mace slammed into an invisible barrier and Sienna stumbled back.

Conryu landed a few feet away. Kai shifted to stand in front of him. The man turned to face Conryu, totally ignoring Sienna who had recovered and was ready to take another run at him.

"Wait a moment, please," Conryu said to Sienna who relaxed a fraction. When it was clear she wasn't about to attack again he asked the stranger, "Who are you?"

"I am the void."

No human throat had ever produced a voice like that. Just the sound of it made Conryu want to puke.

"You know why I'm here?" Conryu asked.

"I know your masters sent you to stop my servants from completing their work. You've set my mission on this world back ten thousand years. But if there's one thing I have, it's time. Someone else will find this place. It doesn't matter where you hide it. Nothing stays gone forever."

"I'm not going to hide the rift," Conryu said. "I'm going to seal it."

The void laughed. "You lack the power."

Black eyes bored into Conryu. "Then again perhaps you don't. I'll offer you a bargain, human. Join me. Become my herald and help me reclaim the universe."

"Why would I do that? I know what you want. If you destroy everything, I'll have nowhere to live. Being alone with you in endless darkness doesn't appeal to me."

"You wouldn't be alone. I have many servants. All will be one in the darkness."

"Why are we talking to this creature?" Sienna demanded. "Let's kill him and be done with it."

The void turned toward her. "Be silent."

Sienna went flying across the cavern.

He turned back to Conryu. "I can offer you power greater than anything you've ever imagined. You will be like a god."

"Power, power, power! Everyone thinks I want power." Conryu's anger grew by the moment. "All I want is to hang out with my friends and enjoy a little peace and quiet without people trying to kill me or blow things up."

The tip of his staff turned brown and the stone of the cavern surged up, wrapping the void in stone. "Now get lost!"

He flicked his wrist and the void went flying in the opposite direction as Sienna.

"That won't hold him for long," Conryu said.

"Do what you must, Chosen," Kai said. "I will hold this monster off for as long as it takes."

*And I will aid her.*

The Reaper's voice surprised him. Before he could respond dark energy crackled around Kai. She vanished and a moment later the sounds of battle came from deep in the cavern.

Putting her out of his mind was the hardest thing Conryu had ever done. He stepped over to the rift and raised both hands. The staff vibrated in his hands.

"I am your conduit," Conryu said. "Erase this abomination."

His awareness vanished as the elemental lords entered his mind.

The chill of the grave settled over Kai as the Reaper's might infused every cell of her being. She had never felt power like that. For an instant she imagined she could defeat any opponent. Even the darkness of the cavern was no obstacle to her now. She spotted the void smashing free of Conryu's stone prison and charged.

Her mace crashed into the man's chest and sent him flying. Impressive as the blow was, she knew it hadn't penetrated. Hitting him was like striking a stone wall. Whatever else the void was, it was tremendously strong.

The man landed lightly on the balls of his feet and turned to face her, no worse for the impact. As she feared, even with the Reaper's help, this enemy was beyond her.

A silent wave of his hand sent a wall of darkness rushing toward her.

Kai vanished into the borderland and emerged a second later directly behind him.

A crashing overhead blow bounced off an invisible barrier and staggered her.

The void turned slowly to face her. "You're a tricky one. I can smell the Reaper's stench all over you. He can't save you. My power is limitless. Perhaps if we fought in Hell, but here, in the seat of my power, you have no hope of winning."

Kai recognized the truth of his words, but it wasn't going to stop her. As long as she had breath in her body, she would keep this monster away from Conryu.

The backhanded blow came so fast she barely got her mace up to take the brunt of the impact. It still sent her flying twenty feet across the cavern.

While still airborne, she slipped into the Hell, righted herself, and reappeared beside him, mace leading.

The spike struck squarely in the void's left eye, penetrated, and gouged out a chunk of flesh and bone.

A dark blast struck her stomach, doubling her over and making her retch.

"An impressive blow." Already the wound was closing. "I didn't think your little toy could break my skin."

Kai scrambled away. Too slowly to avoid a kick that spun her over on her back and sent her sliding across the rough floor. That broke at least one rib and more likely two.

Behind her a light exploded in the darkness.

The void winced. Whatever Conryu was doing, it was starting to work.

"I've wasted enough time on you." A ball of darkness formed in the palm of the man's hand.

Kai dropped into Hell just ahead of the attack.

*Stay strong, Daughter. My chosen has begun closing the rift. The creature will weaken as the spell progresses. Stay strong.*

"Yes, Master."

Kai returned to the mortal realm and smashed the void in the right knee. Bone snapped and he fell part way to the floor. Her opponent was weaker, she could feel it. The knowledge gave her hope. She could do what she had to. She would do it.

The void's snarl was savage, twisting its human host's face into a horrific mask of rage and pain.

Dark beams shot out of his eyes.

Kai dove under them and hammered a second blow into his left arm, snapping it like a twig.

She rolled to her feet and spun to face him again.

"I grow weary of this game, child." Darkness exploded out of the void in every direction. The dark power picked Kai up and carried her along like a leaf caught in a river.

The ride ended when she slammed into the cavern wall, driving the breath from her lungs, and sending her slumping to the floor. When she looked up the void stood over her, darkness crackling around his right hand.

Hopefully she had bought enough time. Kai would miss Conryu but joining her sisters at the Reaper's side would be a fine reward.

Before the final blow could fall, Sienna appeared behind the void and struck the side of his head with all her might.

His head exploded with the force of the impact. The body wobbled and staggered away.

Kai forced herself to her feet, ignoring the pain screaming for her to stay down and not move.

After a few unsteady steps, the headless body straightened and turned toward them. Darkness gathered around it for a second time.

What was it going to take to stop this monster?

The answer came a second later when the dark energy sputtered and the corpse collapsed. Behind them the light had vanished. Conryu had done it. The rift was sealed.

She started to collapse, but strong arms caught her. Warmth and comfort surged into her battered body.

"You did great," Conryu said. "Now let's get out of here."

# EPILOGUE

When Conryu emerged from the cavern beneath Atlantis he found Kanna waiting. She and the ninjas were gathered around the opening. He had healed Kai and Sienna after the battle himself. None of the others appeared badly injured, but he brushed them all with light magic just to be sure. The last thing he needed was for someone to fall now that the battle was won.

The skies were silent, the RAF jets having apparently returned to their base. That was a relief. Getting killed by a misfired missile after surviving a fight with whatever that thing below was would have been a tragedy.

Kanna bowed when he landed. "All the Atlanteans in the city have been eliminated. We lost seven daughters in the process. A great victory given what we faced."

"Yeah, a victory." Exhaustion lay heavily on him after channeling so much power and he still had work to do. "Prepare their bodies for burial. When I've had a day to rest, we'll hold a ceremony to honor them properly. I'll raise the tomb myself back at the monastery. Thank you for everything. All of you."

The ninjas bowed as one and Kanna said, "It was our honor, Chosen. If there's nothing else, we'll return home."

"I think we're good. You've certainly earned the rest. I'll see you tomorrow."

Kanna nodded and they all faded away.

Conryu turned to Kai. "If you want to join them, you've earned the break many times over."

"Where you go, I go, Chosen."

He smiled, not surprised in the least. "What about you, Sienna?"

"Unless I miss my guess, there's still one Atlantean out there. I will hunt him down and finish things once and for all. It's my duty." She raised the mace she'd borrowed. "May I keep this until the hunt is finished?"

"Sure, but don't keep it too long. It would be a shame to lose your hands after all this." He held out his hand and they shook. "Stay safe."

She nodded and vanished into a wind portal.

Now all he had to do was shift the island to a pocket dimension and they could go home. Maybe he'd risk a trip home for some of Giovanni's pizza. The universe knew he'd earned it.

"You should shift to the borderland while I do this."

Kai vanished without a word. Conryu raised his staff for what he hoped would be the last time in a while.

Before he could begin the spell, a portal opened and people began pouring out. There were soldiers, wizards in robes of various colors, and leading them, dressed in all black, was Malice Kincade. Just when he thought nothing could make this day any worse.

"You're trespassing on Alliance property, boy," the old hag said. "Leave now or face the consequences."

She had to be kidding. The combined might of the wizards

and soldiers she'd brought with her couldn't begin to threaten him. What was it with these arrogant assholes? He did all the work and then they imagined they could just swoop in and claim the city for themselves like he had nothing to say about it? They were in for a surprise.

Before he could say anything, another portal opened. This time Jemma led a troop of Kingdom wizards and soldiers. The two groups faced off, Conryu suddenly forgotten.

"This is Kingdom airspace you're violating," Jemma said. "On the king's authority, we are claiming Atlantis."

"We have already claimed it for the Alliance," Malice said. "Unless you're willing to go to war over an empty city, I suggest you back off."

"We have suffered great damage already," Jemma countered. "This city and its secrets are our just compensation. We will fight to keep it."

Both sides snapped weapons up and took aim at each other. The air crackled with readied magic. It wouldn't take much to start another war right here. Conryu was seriously tempted to leave and let them kill each other, but he'd seen enough death over the last few days.

A pulse of dark magic rushed out, washing over both groups, nullifying the gathering magic and reducing everyone's weapons to rust. He stalked over, wrapping himself in defensive magic as he did. They all stared at him as he got closer. He looked from Malice to Jemma and back again.

"Neither of you is claiming Atlantis. I'm shifting it out of the human realm once and for all. Now, unless you want to spend the rest of eternity in a pocket dimension, I suggest you portal back to where you came from."

Jemma and Malice both opened their mouths to protest.

Conryu cut them off immediately. "This isn't a debate. I'm

exhausted and pissed. Anyone still in this city when I reach ten is going for a long, one-way trip. One!"

Jemma and Malice glared at him then at each other before ordering portals opened. He reached eight before they closed. Alone again, he resumed his interrupted spell. Much like sealing the rift, he wasn't fully in control of the magic as a great, white dome slowly formed around the city.

When it was fully enclosed, he had a vague sense of movement, then complete stillness. All around was nothing but white emptiness. For a moment he thought he was in Heaven, but there was no sense of warmth or welcome. Wherever he was, hopefully it would be safe.

*It will be,* the Reaper said in an ominous – more than ominous – tone.

*Indeed, we shall make certain of it,* the Goddess agreed.

If the two of them were in agreement about something, he could rest easy knowing it was done. Maybe now he could enjoy a little peace and quiet.

For a little while at least.

## AUTHOR NOTE

Hello Everyone,

I hope you all enjoyed reading the next installment of Conryu's adventures. If you'd like to know when my next book is coming out you can hope over to my website and join my newsletter. I'd love to have you.

James

# ABOUT THE AUTHOR

James E. Wisher is a writer of science fiction and fantasy novels. He's been writing since high school and reading everything he could get his hands on for as long as he can remember.

*To learn more:*
www.jamesewisher.com
james@jamesewisher.com

ALSO BY JAMES E WISHER

The Dragonspire Chronicles
The Black Egg
The Mysterious Coin
The Dragons' Graveyard
The Slave War
The Sunken Tower
The Dragon Empress

Soul Force Saga
Disciples of the Horned One Trilogy:
Darkness Rising
Raging Sea and Trembling Earth
Harvest of Souls
Disciples of the Horned One Omnibus
Chains of the Fallen Arc:
Dreaming in the Dark
On Blackened Wings
Chains of the Fallen Omnibus
Knight of the Red Dragon

The Aegis of Merlin:
The Impossible Wizard
The Awakening
The Chimera Jar

The Raven's Shadow
Escape From the Dragon Czar
Wrath of the Dragon Czar
The Four Nations Tournament
Death Incarnate
Atlantis Rising
Aegis of Merlin Omnibus Vol 1.
Aegis of Merlin Omnibus Vol 2.
The Complete Aegis of Merlin Omnibus

Other Fantasy Novels:
The Squire
Death and Honor Omnibus

The Rogue Star Series:
Children of Darkness
Children of the Void
Children of Junk
Rogue Star Omnibus Vol. 1
Children of the Black Ship

Made in the USA
Monee, IL
12 April 2021